"What the h[...] doing?" she demanded, launching herself at him.

"I wouldn't advise you do that again." Seizing hold of her wrists, he held her in front of him. His gaze slipped to her lips. The urge to ravage them overwhelmed him.

"Let go of me, Heath," she warned him. Her voice was shaking. Her eyes were dark. Her lips were parted—

Control kicked in. He lifted his hands away. "Get off my property," he said.

"You don't frighten me," she muttered, rubbing her wrists as she pulled away.

But he had frightened her. Bronte had feared her reaction to him. The snap of static between them had surprised him. This was no ordinary reunion, he reflected as she began bringing her tent down. The redheaded tomboy and the bad boy from the city had enjoyed some high-voltage scraps in the past, and it appeared that passion hadn't abated. But it had changed, Heath reflected. Bronte felt slight and vulnerable beneath his hands. She was all grown up now, and her scent of soap and damp grass had grazed his senses, leaving an impression he would find hard to shake off.

SUSAN STEPHENS was a professional singer before meeting her husband on the tiny Mediterranean island of Malta. In true Harlequin Presents style, they met on Monday, became engaged on Friday and were married three months later. Almost thirty years and three children later, they are still in love. (Susan does not advise her children to return home one day with a similar story, as she may not take the news with the same fortitude as her own mother!)

Susan had written several nonfiction books when fate took a hand. At a charity costume ball there was an after-dinner auction. One of the lots, "Spend a Day with an Author", had been donated by Harlequin Presents author Penny Jordan. Susan's husband bought this lot and Penny was to become not just a great friend, but a wonderful mentor who encouraged Susan to write romance.

Susan loves her family, her pets, her friends and her writing. She enjoys entertaining, travel and going to the theater. She reads, cooks and plays the piano to relax, and can occasionally be found throwing herself off mountains on a pair of skis or galloping through the countryside.

Visit Susan's website, www.susanstephens.net.

Other titles by Susan Stephens available in ebook:

Harlequin Presents

Harlequin Presents Extra

WORKING WITH THE ENEMY

SUSAN STEPHENS

~ **Risky Business** ~

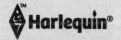

TORONTO NEW YORK LONDON
AMSTERDAM PARIS SYDNEY HAMBURG
STOCKHOLM ATHENS TOKYO MILAN MADRID
PRAGUE WARSAW BUDAPEST AUCKLAND

Recycling programs
for this product may
not exist in your area.

ISBN-13: 978-0-373-52851-6

WORKING WITH THE ENEMY

Originally published in the U.K. as THE BIG, BAD BOSS

First North American Publication 2012

Copyright © 2011 Susan Stephens

www.Harlequin.com

Printed in U.S.A.

WORKING WITH
THE ENEMY

CHAPTER ONE

'*DAWN. and in front of us the idyllic English country scene. Smell that grass. Look at that thin stream of sunlight driving night-shadows down the velvet hills—*'

How long did he have to stay here?

With an exasperated roar, Heath flipped channels, silencing the farming programme. All he'd smelled so far was cow dung. And it was raining.

Resting his chin on one arm, he slammed his foot down on the accelerator. The Lamborghini roared drowning out the birdsong. Perfect. He missed the concrete jungle—no smells, no mud, no cranky plumbing. Why Uncle Harry had left him a run-down country estate remained a mystery. Heath was allergic to the country—to anything that didn't come with dot-com attached. His empire had been built in a bedroom. What did he need all this for?

And it was only after asking himself that question that he spotted the tent someone had erected on a mossy bank just inside the gates…spotted the small pink feet sticking out of the entrance. Forget hating the place. He felt proprietorial suddenly. What would he do if someone pitched a tent outside the front door of his London home?

Stopping the car, he climbed out. Striding up to the tent, he unzipped it.

A yelp of surprise ripped through the steady drum of falling rain. Standing back, he folded his arms, waiting for developments. He didn't have long to wait. A strident pixie crawled out, screaming at him that it was the middle of the night as she sprang to her feet. Red hair flying, she stood like an irate stick insect telling him what she thought of him in language as colourful as the clothes she was frantically tugging on—a camouflage top, and shot-off purple leggings that displayed her tiny feet. One furious glance at his car and he was responsible for everything from frightening the local wildlife to global warming, apparently, until finally, having got over the shock of being so rudely awakened, she gulped, took a breath, and exclaimed, 'Heath Stamp…' Clapping a hand to her chest, she stared at him as if she couldn't believe her eyes.

'Bronte Foster-Jenkins,' he murmured, taking her in.

'I've been expecting you—'

'So I see,' he said, glancing at the tent.

Expecting Heath to arrive? Yes, but not her reaction to it. He wasn't supposed to arrive at dawn, either. Around midday, the postmistress in the village had suggested. Heath Stamp, hip, slick, rugged, tough, and even better looking than his most recent images in the press suggested. This was a vastly improved version of someone she'd dreamed about for thirteen years, two months, six hours, and—

'You do know you're trespassing, Bronte?'

And as delightful as ever.

The years melted away. They were at loggerheads immediately. She had to remind herself Heath was no longer a wild youth who'd been locked up for bare-knuckle fighting, and who used to visit Hebers Ghyll on a release programme, but a successful Internet entrepreneur and the new owner of Hebers Ghyll, the country estate where Bronte had grown up, and where her mother had been the housekeeper and her father the gamekeeper. 'The estate has been deserted for weeks now—'

'And that's an excuse for breaking in?'

'The gates were open. Everything's gone to pot,' she told him angrily.

'And that's my fault?'

'You own it. You tell me.' Heath's inheritance had a special hold on her heart for all sorts of reasons, not least of which she considered the estate her second home.

While Heath had gained nothing in charm, Bronte registered as he turned his back, he clearly still couldn't care less what people thought of him. He never had.

He'd walked off to give them both space. Seeing Bronte again had floored him. Since the first time he had visited the estate—where ironically his real-life uncle Harry had used to run a rehabilitation centre for out-of-control youths—there had been something between him and Bronte, something that drew the good girl to the dark side. He'd tried to steer clear, not wanting to taint her. But he would think about her when he sat alone and stared at his bruised knuckles. She was light to his darkness. Back then Bronte had represented everything that was pure, fun and happy, while he was the youth from the gutter who met every challenge with his fists. He'd worshipped her from afar, had she only known it. That buzz between them surely should have died by now.

'That tree was struck by lightning, and no one's moved it,' she said, reclaiming his attention.

He hadn't even realised he'd been staring at the old tree, but now he remembered Uncle Harry telling him that it had stood on the estate for centuries.

'It'll stay there until it rots, I suppose,' she flared.

'I'll have it moved.' He shrugged. 'Maybe have something planted in its place.'

'It would mean more if you did it.'

He threw her a glance, warning her not to push it. But she would. She always had. Bronte loved a campaign whether it was free the chickens, or somewhere for the local youth to hang out.

'And just think of all the free firewood,' she said casually.

She was working on him. When hadn't she? And now it all came flooding back—what she'd done for him—and how he used to envy Bronte her simple life on the estate with her happy family. He'd felt a hungry desperation to share what they had but had never allowed them to draw him in, in case he spoiled it. He'd spoiled everything back then.

And now?

He was still hard and contained.

And Hebers Ghyll?

Was in the pending file.

And Bronte?

Heath raked his hair with impatience.

This was all happening too fast, way too fast. She hadn't expected to feel as shaken as this when she saw Heath again. Heading for the shelter of some trees where the thick green canopy acted like a giant umbrella, she sucked in some deep steadying breaths. She had to remind herself why she was here—to find out what

Heath's plans for the estate were. 'I heard the new owner was going to break up the estate—'

'And?'

'You can't.' Bronte's heart picked up pace as Heath came to join her beneath the branches. 'You don't know enough about the area as it is today. You don't know how desperate people are for jobs. You haven't been near the place for years—'

'And you have?'

Bronte's cheeks flared red. Yes, she'd been away, but her travels had been geared towards putting what she had learned at college into practice. As a child she had dogged Uncle Harry's footsteps, trying to be useful and asking him endless questions about Hebers Ghyll. He'd said she was a good lieutenant and might make a decent estate manager one day if she worked hard enough. When she left school Uncle Harry had paid for her to go to college to study estate management. 'I've been away recently,' she conceded, 'but apart from that I've lived on the estate all my life.'

'So, what are you saying, Bronte? You're the only one who cares about Hebers Ghyll?' Heath's chin dipped a warning.

'Well, do you care,' Bronte exclaimed with frustration, 'beyond its value?'

'I'd be foolish not to care about its value.'

'But there's so much more than money here.' And she had been prepared to camp out on the road leading up to the old house for as long as it took to prove that to him. 'Why else do you think I scrabbled round my parents' attic to find the old tent?' Heath's dark gaze flashed a warning, which she ignored. 'Do you think I like camping out in the rain?'

'I don't know what you like.'

The gulf between them yawned. It might have been easier to explain and convince Heath if she had seen him recently. The shock of seeing him again after all these years was something she hadn't anticipated. It wasn't how tall he was, or how good-looking—it was the aura of danger and unapologetic masculinity she found so unnerving.

'So, Bronte,' Heath observed in the laid-back husky voice that had always made her toes curl with excitement, 'what can I do for you?'

She exhaled, refusing to think about it. 'By the time I got back here, Heath, Uncle Harry was dead and everything was in a mess. No one on the estate or in the village had a clue what was going to happen—or whether they still had jobs—'

'And your parents?' Heath prompted.

She guessed Heath already knew the answer to that. The lawyers would have filled him in on what had happened to the staff at Hebers Ghyll. 'I can only think Uncle Harry must have realised he was gravely ill, because he gave my parents some money before he died. He told them to take a break—to fulfil their lifetime's ambition of travelling the world.' She was hugging herself for reassurance, Bronte realised, releasing her arms. It was hard to launch a cogent argument in defence of the estate while Heath was staring at her so intently. He knew her too well. Even after all this time he could sense what she wasn't saying. He could sense how she felt. They had always been uncannily connected, though when Heath had first arrived on the estate she'd been more concerned that the ruffian Uncle Harry was trying to tame would tear the head off her dolls. The feeling Heath inspired in her now was very different. 'I can't believe you're the Master of Hebers Ghyll,' she said, shaking her head.

'And you don't like the idea?'

'I didn't say that—'

'You didn't have to. Perhaps you think Uncle Harry should have left his estate to you—'

'No,' Bronte exclaimed indignantly. 'That never occurred to me. You're his nephew, Heath. I'm only the housekeeper's daughter—'

'Who walked in here and made herself at home.' He glanced at her tent.

'The gates were open. Ask your estate manager if you don't believe me.'

'That man was employed by Uncle Harry's executors and no longer works for me.'

'Well, whoever he was…' Bronte's voice faded when she realised Heath had only owned the estate five minutes and had already sacked one member of staff.

'He was a waste of space,' Heath rapped. 'And replaceable.'

Heath unnerved her. Was everyone replaceable in Heath's world?

'If there are so many people clamouring for jobs in the area,' he said, reclaiming her attention, 'it shouldn't take me long to find another man—'

'Or a woman.'

Heath huffed a humourless laugh. 'Still the same Bronte.'

The last time they'd had this sort of stand-off she'd been twelve and Heath fifteen, difficult ages for both of them, impossible to find common ground. Those years had changed nothing, Bronte registered, conscious of her furiously erect nipples beneath the flimsy top. She casually folded her arms across her chest. 'When can we meet for a proper talk?'

'When you approach me through the proper channels.'

'I tried to call you, but your PA wouldn't put me through. I'm only here now because I was determined to talk to you.'

'You? Determined, Bronte?' The first glint of humour broke through Heath's fierce façade.

'Someone had to find out what was going on.'

'And as usual that someone's you?'

'I offered to be a spokesperson.'

'You offered?' Heath pulled back his head to look at her through narrowed storm-grey eyes. 'What a surprise.'

'So, are you going to tell me what your plans are for the estate?' Why wouldn't her pulse slow down?

Because of that aura of bad-boy danger surrounding Heath, her inner voice supplied. The years hadn't changed it—and they certainly hadn't diminished it.

'I'll tell you what I'm going to do,' Heath said.

'Yes?' She held her ground tensely as he strolled towards her.

'This place is a mess,' he said, his gesture taking in broken fences, crumbling walls and overgrown hedgerows, 'and probate took time. But I'm here now. What happens next?' She swallowed deep as he looked down at her. 'I make an assessment.'

'That's it?' she whispered, hypnotised by his eyes.

'That's it,' Heath confirmed harshly, wheeling away. 'You haven't been inside the house yet, I take it?'

Bronte's brave front faltered. 'No. I came straight here.' Now her imagination had raced into overdrive. The estate comprised a hall and a broken-down castle as well as a great deal of land. Uncle Harry had lived at the hall, and had always kept it as well as he could afford to—which wasn't very well, but if anything was less than perfect it was only because Uncle Harry spent so much of his money helping others. The original stained-glass windows were beautiful, she remembered, and there was a wonderful wood-panelled library where the log fire was always burning, and a spotless, if anti-quated, kitchen, which had been her mother's domain. Was all that changed? 'What's happened, Heath?' she said anxiously. 'Can I help?'

'What can you do?' he said.

She was surprised he had to ask. And hurt that he had. It made her more determined than ever to find out what Heath's true intentions were. 'Rumours say you've already sold the Hebers Ghyll estate on—'

'Anything else?' Heath demanded, folding his power-ful arms across his chest.

His eyes were every bit as beautiful as she remem-bered and just as cold. She shook herself round. 'And bulldozers—I heard talk of bulldozers.' There was no point sugar-coating this. She might just as well confront him with the lot. 'One rumour said you were going to bring in a wrecking crew to knock everything down, and then you'd build a shopping centre—'

'And what if I did?'

Panic hit her at the thought that he might—that he could—that he had every right to. 'What about Uncle Harry?'

'Uncle Harry's dead.'

Heath might as well have stabbed a knife through her heart. Heath had always been closed off to feelings except on those rare occasions when he had lightened up in front of Bronte or Uncle Harry. Sometimes she won-dered if they were the only people he had ever opened up to. And that was a memory so faint she couldn't believe it had ever happened now. 'For goodness' sake, Heath, you're his nephew—don't you feel anything?' To hell with the job she had intended to apply for. 'Does Hebers Ghyll mean anything to you? Don't you remember what Uncle Harry used to do—?'

'For kids like me?' Heath interrupted her coldly. She'd taken him back to the past, and his father, Uncle Harry's wastrel brother—the poor relation with the taste for violence. Only at the court's insistence had his father agreed to a period of rehabilitation for Heath at Hebers Ghyll under Uncle Harry's direction. And how he'd fought it. Heath had thrown Uncle Harry's kindness back in his face. A fact he'd spent his adult life regretting.

'You know I didn't mean that,' Bronte assured him. 'Uncle Harry loved having you around. You must have known you were the son he never had?'

'Don't use those tactics on me, Bronte.'

'Tactics?' she exploded. 'I'm not using tactics. I'm telling you the truth. Don't pretend you don't care, Heath. I know you better than that—'

'You know me?' he snarled, dipping his chin.

'Yes. I know you,' she argued stubbornly, refusing to back down.

'You knew me then,' he said. And he didn't like reminders of then.

'I don't want to fight with you, Heath.'

Her voice had turned softer. Bronte backing down? That had to be a first. Had the years smoothed her out? Remembering her welcome, he guessed not. 'Apology accepted,' he said. But even as their eyes met and held he knew this small concession was the first step on the road to damnation, the first nod to his libido. Bronte was still as attractive as ever—more so, when she was all fired up.

'It's important Uncle Harry's work here continue,' she told him, her brow creasing with passion. 'And with you at the helm, Heath,' she added with less conviction.

His senses stirred. She was magnificent with those green eyes blazing and that dainty jaw jutting. She was unflinching. Boudicca of the Yorkshire moors. But she was also uneasy and unsure of him. She was unsure of what he'd do. Thinking back to what seemed like another life to him now, he couldn't blame her. 'You'll be the first to know when I make my decision. But know this: I don't do weekends. I don't do holidays. And I don't need a country house. You work it out.'

'I think that answers my question,' The green gaze remained steady on his face.

'If you care so much about Hebers Gyll, what are you going to do about it?' he said, turning the tables on her.

'I won't walk away without a fight.'

He didn't doubt it. 'And in practical terms?'

She tilted her chin at a determined angle. 'Whether or not you keep the estate, I'm going to apply for the job of estate manager.'

He laughed out loud. She really had surprised him now. 'Making jam tarts with your mother at the kitchen table hardly qualifies you for that.'

'You're not the only one to have made something of yourself, Heath,' she fired back. 'I have qualifications in estate management—and I've travelled the world, studying how vast tracts of land and properties like this can be managed successfully.'

Now she had his interest.

'It's only natural I want to know what your plans are,'

she insisted. 'I don't want to be wasting my pitch on the wrong man.' Out came the chin.

'My plans are no business of yours.' He stopped admiring her when it occurred to him that Bronte wanted something that belonged to him. Or at least, she wanted control of Hebers Ghyll, which amounted to the same thing. It was a challenge he couldn't ignore. A lot of water had passed under the bridge since he'd been a hard, fighting, rebellious youth and Bronte the housekeeper's prim little daughter sneaking out to see him, hiding in the shadows, thinking he didn't know she was there, but he hadn't changed when it came to protecting what was his. 'If you want me to make time to see you, clear up this mess and get off my property.' He pointed to the area around her tent, which, in fairness, was neat. Bronte had always respected the countryside.

'You promised we'd talk.'

'I'll make a start, shall I?' he said, losing patience.

She exclaimed with surprise when he swooped on a tent peg and jerked it out. 'What the hell do you think you're doing?' she demanded, launching herself at him.

'I wouldn't advise you do that again.' Seizing hold of her wrists, he held her in front of him. His gaze slipping to her parted lips. The urge to ravage them overwhelmed him.

'Let go of me, Heath,' she warned him. Her voice was shaking. Her eyes were dark. Her lips were parted—

Control kicked in. He lifted his hands away. 'Remove the tent,' he said.

'You don't frighten me,' she muttered, rubbing her wrists as she pulled away.

But he had frightened her. Bronte had feared her reaction to him. The snap of static between them had surprised him. This was no ordinary reunion, he reflected as she began bringing her tent down. The redhead tomboy and the bad boy from the city had enjoyed some high voltage scraps in the past, and it appeared that passion hadn't abated. But it had changed, Heath reflected. Bronte had felt slight and vulnerable beneath his hands. She was all grown-up now, and her scent of soap and damp grass had grazed his senses, leaving an impression he would find hard to shake off.

CHAPTER TWO

HEATH STAMP was back. She kept repeating the mantra in her head as if that were going to make it easier for her to be close to him without quivering like a doe on heat. She had been expecting Heath, and had thought she was well prepared for this first encounter, but nothing could have prepared her for feeling so vulnerable, so aware and aroused.

'Get a move on, Bronte.'

'I'm moving as fast as I can.'

'Good, because some of us have work to do.'

'Yeah, me too,' Bronte muttered tensely. She had sorted herself out with a part-time office job in the area while she was still away on her travels—it was just sheer luck Heath had chosen to arrive at the weekend.

'Come on, come on,' he urged impatiently. 'I have to get back to London—'

'We all have things to do, Heath.'

The rain had stopped and Heath was pacing. He had always suffered energy overload and that force was pinging off him now. She wouldn't be taking so long if he didn't look so good. Fantasies she could handle, but this much reality was a problem. Heath's hair had always been thick and strong, but he'd grown it longer and it caressed his strong, tanned neck, curling over the collar of his shirt, and was every bit as wayward as she remembered. Waves caught on his sharply etched cheeks where his black stubble had won the razor war, and, though he might not have fought with his fists for many years, Heath was still built, still tanned, and, apart from the car, he didn't flash his wealth, which she liked. His clothes were designed for practicality rather than to impress—banged-up jeans worn thin and pale over the place where a nice girl shouldn't look, and boots comfortably worn in. Heath had sexy feet, she remembered from those times years back when she had spied on him swimming in the lake—

'Have you turned into a pillar of salt? Or is there a chance we might get out of here today, Bronte?'

'Are you still there?' she retorted, lavishing what Heath used to call her paint-stripping stare on him. The old banter starting up between them had stirred her fighting spirit—

Until Heath reminded her why she was here.

'Are you serious about trying out for the job of estate manager?'

'Of course I am.' She shot to her feet, realising how slender a thread her hopes were pinned on. 'And if you decide not to keep the property I hope you'll put in a good word for me with the new owner.'

'Why would I do that when I don't even know what you can do? Okay, I admit I'm intrigued by what you told me about your training and your travels. But what makes you think you're the right person for this job?'

'I know I am,' she said stubbornly. 'All I'm asking for is a fair hearing.'

'And if I give you one?'

'You can make up your mind then. Maybe give me a trial?' She knew she was pushing it, but what the hell?

Heath said nothing for a moment, and then his lips tugged in a faint, mocking smile. 'If I keep the estate I'll bear your offer in mind.'

It was enough—it was something. Heath never made an impulsive decision, Bronte remembered—that was her department.

'Go home now, Bronte. You've still got your parents' cottage to go to, I take it?'

'They wouldn't sell that.' There was an edge of defiance in her voice. 'Thank goodness they owned it—I heard you bought out all the tenancies.'

'Another of those rumours?' Heath's eyes turned black. 'It didn't occur to you people might want to sell to me? Or that this was their opportunity to do something new with their lives—like your parents?'

'And you wanted a fresh page?'

Heath didn't even try to put a gloss on what he'd done. 'No,' he argued. 'I wanted a clear field so there wouldn't be any complications if and when I choose to sell. What's the matter with you, Bronte?' His face had turned coolly assessing. 'Can't you bear to think of me living at the hall?'

'That's not it at all.'

'Then why don't you smile and be happy for me?'

'I am happy for you, Heath.'

'And you think we could work together?' he said with a mocking edge to his voice.

'I'd find a way.'

'That's big of you,' he said coolly.

Most people would be champing at the bit for a chance to work with Heath Stamp, Bronte realised, turning her back on him as she returned to her packing. She could only hazard a guess at the number of applications Heath would receive if he decided to keep the estate on and threw a recruitment ad out there. Everyone loved a success story in the hope that some of the gold dust would rub off on them—and Heath had gold dust to spare. His story read like a film—the poor boy rejecting a hand up from a well-meaning uncle who just happened to be one of England's biggest landowners, only for the boy to achieve success in his own right and then go on to inherit the uncle's estate anyway. No wonder it had made the headlines. But was she the only one out of step here? Heath had always been open about his dislike of the countryside—everything moved too slowly for him and things took too long to grow, she remembered him snarling at her when she had begged him to stay.

So, could she work with him?

Good question. The thought of seeing Heath on a regular basis might send a warm dart of honey to her core, but when her imagination supplied the fantasy detail, which included a doting lover called Heath and a compliant young girl called Bronte, she knew it was never going to happen, so she just said coolly, 'I'll stay in touch.'

Heath Stamp, Master of Hebers Ghyll? However much Heath teased her with the prospect, she just couldn't see it.

The years had moulded and enhanced Bronte—brought her into clearer focus. She was still the same dreamer who steadfastly refused to learn the meaning of the word no. She was every bit as stubborn and determined as he remembered—if not more so. Only Bronte could come up with the crazy notion that by camping inside the gates she could scope out the new owner of the estate— potentially waylay the new owner, and then insist they consider her for the job of estate manager. Nerve? Oh, yes. Bronte had nerve—and she had never been short of ideas, or the brio to back them up.

'Go away, Heath,' she snapped when he went to give her a hand with the groundsheet. 'I can do this by myself.'

'I don't doubt it. I just want to make sure you don't leave anything behind.'

'So I have no excuse to come back?'

Looks clashed. Eyes darkened. Something else for him to think about. 'Just do it, will you?'

'Don't worry—I've got no reason to hang around here.' She threw him a disdainful look. 'Why on earth would I?'

A million and one reasons, Bronte thought, feeling all mixed up inside. She didn't want to go—she didn't want to stay. It didn't help she'd brought so much stuff and it was taking so long to fit it back in her rucksack. She could feel the heat of Heath's stare on her back. And low in her belly the dreamweaver was working—

'Come on. Get a move on, Bronte.'

'Yes, master—'

'Less of it—and more packing,' Heath snapped.

She was seething with frustration. Was this the same girl who had the right training for this job, as well as great qualifications? The girl who had worked her way round the world to make doubly sure she would be ready to apply for a job on the estate when she got back? And with the biggest job of all on offer, was she going to blow it now because she couldn't see further than Heath? Bite your lip, Bronte, was the best piece of advice to follow. There was too much at stake to do anything else. She should have rung the lawyers the moment she was back in the country and avoided this meeting. She should have approached things in the usual way.

Could anything be usual where Heath was concerned?

If she had given him warning of her intentions, her best guess was Heath wouldn't have turned up—or he'd make sure to be permanently unavailable at his office. But Hebers Ghyll needed him—needed Heath's golden touch *and* his money. She had to put her personal feelings to one side and persuade him to keep the estate together and not to sell or demolish any of the old buildings in the 'so called' name of progress.

'You won't be very comfortable without this,' he observed, toeing the edge of her groundsheet.

As she started to roll it up the scent of damp earth stirred her memories. Her parents had met and fallen in love at Hebers Ghyll, which gave it a sort of magic. The freedom of the fields when she'd been a child—somewhere to curl up with a book and lose herself—all the things that had made her feel safe and secure had gone, because every last inch of this damp, sweet-smelling ground belonged to Heath now, and there wasn't a thing she could do about it.

'Why did you bring all this?' Heath had come to stand very close.

She lifted her head and stared into the critical gaze, wishing there were some warmth in it—some recognition that they had been friends once. 'I didn't know how long I'd have to wait for you,' she said truthfully.

'You were only sure that you would,' Heath commented without expression.

'That's right,' she said, blazing defiance into his eyes.

'Nothing changes, does it, Bronte?'

'Some things do,' she said. Let him know how she felt. 'With the future of the village at stake I had no alternative, Heath. No one sleeps on the ground out of choice.'

She could have bitten off her tongue. Heath's success had been forged out of a combustible mix of fiery determination and uncompromising poverty. He knew very well what it was like to sleep on the ground. Uncle Harry had told her once his parents used to lock him out when he was a child while they went to the pub, and if they were home late or not at all Heath had to do the best he could to find shelter. 'Heath, I'm sorry—'

With a shake of his head he closed the subject.

Sleeping on park benches to escape the violence at home had done nothing to soften him, Bronte reflected, returning to her packing. And that stint in jail must have knocked all human feeling out of him. Yes, and what would a man like that know or care about the countryside—or the legacy he had inherited? 'Heath,' she pleaded softly, sitting back on her haunches. 'You will give this place a chance, won't you?'

He surveyed her steadily through steel-grey eyes. 'I'm here to see what can be done, Bronte. And if I want to do it.'

'That's not enough.'

Heath huffed. 'It's all you're getting.'

'If you even think of turning your back on Hebers Ghyll I'll fight you every inch of the way.'

'Bare knuckle or Queensberry Rules?'

She stared at him intently for a moment. She hardly dared to hope that was a flicker of the old humour, but in the unlikely event that it was she wasn't going to cause a storm and blow it out.

'What about those cooking pots, Bronte?' Heath demanded. 'Am I supposed to clear them up? If you don't get a move on I'll fetch the tractor and shift them myself.'

'The tractor?' she repeated witheringly. 'Here is a man,' she informed the trees, 'whose knowledge of the countryside would fit comfortably on the head of a pin with room for angels to dance in a ring. Heath Stamp—' she introduced him with a theatrical gesture '—creator of imaginary worlds contained in neat square boxes— computers that can be conveniently switched off, and don't have to be milked twice a day.' She turned to Heath. 'What would you know about driving a tractor?'

'More than you know.'

'It would have to be more than I know—' But now Heath's hand was in the small of her back and everything dissolved in a flood of sensation. Jerking away, she bent down to pick up the overloaded pack.

'Let me help you—'

'Go away.'

'Bronte—'

Heath waited a moment and then he strode off.

She turned to watch him go, still heated and furious— desperate for him to go, and longing for him to stay. She couldn't believe how badly this much-longed-for reunion had gone. Heath, and that firm mouth—how she hated it. She hated the confident swagger of his walk, and those taut, powerful hips. She hated his manner, which was both cool and hot, and infinitely disturbing, as well as blatantly unavailable—at least, to her. Heath might have his own brand of rugged charm, but according to the press he attracted glamorous, elegant women—women who decorated Heath's life without ever becoming part of it—

She nearly jumped out of her skin when he reappeared through the trees.

'Okay,' he said curtly, 'I can't abandon you here. Give me that pack.'

Heath didn't wait for her reply. Wrestling the pack from her shoulders, he stalked off with it, leaving her stunned by the brief and definitely unintentional brushing of their bodies. 'Hey—come back here,' she yelled, coming to as Heath and her backpack disappeared through the trees.

She might as well have been talking to herself. Grinding her jaw, she started after him. Heath had never been a man to mess about with, but she wasn't a girl to back down. Mud sucked at her trainers as she started to run. Wet leaves slapped at her face. Who could keep up with Heath? Bronte reasoned when she was forced to stop and catch her breath. Heath had always been a one-man powerhouse since the day he sewed the seeds of his empire on a computer he'd hidden in his bedroom, where damp dappled the walls and the only green Heath ever saw was the mould that flourished there. Bad start in life, maybe, but this city boy was fit—fitter than she was. Catching sight of Heath through the trees, she found a fresh burst of energy. He had always moved fast. The first time Heath had hit the headlines was because of the speed with which he had turned his old family home into an Internet café for the whole neighbourhood to use. The reporters had latched onto the fact that, far from turning his back on his miserable start in life, when Heath made money he celebrated his background, using his story to inspire others to follow his example and make the best of what they had. Leaning one hand against a tree trunk, she took another breather. So Heath Stamp was a saint, but right now that didn't make her like him any better.

But if he could be persuaded to do the same for Hebers Ghyll the estate might stand a chance...

With this thought propelling her forward she got a rush of energy—right up to the moment when Heath yelled, 'I'm dumping this pack on the road, Bronte. After that, you're on your own.'

So much charm in one man. Blowing out an angry breath, she wiped the mud off her face with the back of her hand and pushed on. When she finally caught up to him Heath was the epitome of cool. He hadn't even broken sweat.

'I'd give you a lift...' His sardonic gaze ran over her mud-blackened clothes.

'Save it, Heath. You wouldn't want to dirty your car.'

Heath threw her one of his looks. 'Your rucksack wouldn't fit in the boot.'

'Lucky you.' Heath's sexy mouth was mocking her. His eyes were too. Hefting the pack up, she turned her back on him and marched away.

CHAPTER THREE

HE COULDN'T believe how screwed up inside Bronte made him feel. And this didn't help. Heath was staring at the old hall, seeing it for the first time through adult eyes. He had thought he knew it well, and that he remembered every detail. But he hadn't bargained for the memories flooding in.

Thankfully, he was alone. There had been a moment just then when, despite priding himself on his fitness. It had felt as if his chest were in a vice. He could hear police sirens in his head. He could hear his mother screaming at his father not to hit her. He could see a small boy locked out of the house until his parents got home late at night, relieving himself against the back wall, the neighbours shouting at him. And he could feel the difference here at Hebers Ghyll all over again: the stability; the kindness shown to him; the patience that people had given a boy who believed he deserved none, the care he had so badly needed. He felt that same hunger again—not just the hunger for food, but the hunger for something different. He hadn't even known what was driving him back then. But he did know that here at Hebers Ghyll was where anger had started to grow like a weed twining round him as he turned from bewildered child into disaffected youth. The anger had been thick and fast and ugly, and he had expressed it with his fists.

If he stayed very still the echoes of those years were stronger—the first time he'd been to Hebers Ghyll he'd felt resentful and out of place. Seeing Bronte again had rubbed salt in that wound. The first time he'd seen her, his jaw had dropped to think such innocence existed—it was the first time he realised not every family was at war.

But however much Bronte wanted him to come back to Hebers Ghyll and work some sort of miracle—and she did—he couldn't shake off that old certainty that he didn't belong here. Who would want to be reminded of his past—of what he'd been—of what he could be? Back then there had only been one certainty—one over-riding conviction. He could never be good enough for Bronte.

And now?

She had taught him to read, for God's sake.

Shame washed over him as he remembered. It made him want to jump in the car, drive home to London and never come back. Why shouldn't he do just that? He'd put this place on the market—leave the past where it belonged, buried deep in the countryside at Hebers Ghyll.

Decision made, he headed back to the car, but then a sound stopped him dead in his tracks. It jerked him back into the present even as it threw him into the past. He turned and stared at the old bell Uncle Harry had hung outside the front door so he could call the bad boys in for supper. Heath's mouth twisted as he shook his head. Whatever he thought about it, the past wasn't ready to let him go yet. Leaving the bell to its capricious dance, he jogged up the steps to the front door and let himself in.

He felt a sort of grief mixed up with guilt land heavily inside him as he stared around the entrance hall. How could this have happened so quickly?

What had he expected? A log fire blazing, the smell of freshly baked bread? There was no one living here—no one had been living here for months. The scent of pine and wood-smoke he remembered belonged to another, happier era. The air was stale now, and cold, and stank of damp. He walked around—touching, listening, remembering...

If there was one thing Uncle Harry had insisted on, it was that the log fire was kept burning so that visitors felt welcome. And the table where his uncle had taught him the fundamentals of chess before Heath crossed over to the dark side—where was that? Where was the board? Where were the chess pieces?

Melancholy washed over him and it was an emotion he had never thought to feel here. Bronte was right to think he had arrived with the sole intention of developing the property and selling it on to make a quick profit—until she had planted that seed of doubt in his head, reminding him of the old man who had done so much for both of them. Credit for his artistic flair and business savvy, Heath could claim, but the fuel that had fired his hunger to do better had been all Uncle Harry.

Raking his hair as he looked around, he thought the word dilapidation didn't even begin to cover this. Bottom line? He didn't have time for Hebers Ghyll. His life, his work—everything—was in London. His impressive-sounding inheritance was little more than a ruin—a hall, with a tumble-down castle in the grounds, whose foundations had been laid in Norman times, and whose structure had been added to over the years with a mixed degree of success.

Make that heavy on the failure, Heath thought as he leaned his shoulder against a wall and heard it grumble. He had to wonder what Uncle Harry had been thinking on the day the old man had written his will. It was common knowledge Heath hated the countryside. Even as a youth he'd scorned the idea that owning a castle was grand; it was just a larger acreage of slum to him—still was. There was nothing here but rotten wood and cracks and holes, and leaking radiators.

But at least he was no stranger to this sort of mess...

His talent was in inventing computer games and running a company soon to go global, but his hobby was working with his hands. It wouldn't be the first time he'd called a team together to work on the renovation of an ancient building.

Yes, but this was a huge project. He gave himself a reality check as he continued his inspection. Rubbing a pane of glass with his sleeve, he peered through an upstairs window...and thought about the dormitory Uncle Harry had set up in the barn for Heath and the other boys from the detention centre. They'd had fun—not that Heath would have admitted it at the time. They'd told ghost stories late into the night, trying to spook each other—and during the day they'd ridden bareback on the ponies, or risked their lives wrestling bullocks. The space and silence had got to him, but the village hadn't been without its attractions. A challenge from the leader of the country lads with their burnished skin and glossy hair had led to a fight and Heath had established quite a reputation for himself. When he returned to the city he took things one disastrous step further, fighting for cash in dank, dark cellars—until the authorities caught up with him. After a chase the police had arrested him here, of all places—at Hebers Ghyll. He'd returned like a homing pigeon, he realised now. He'd gone back to the detention centre for a longer stretch.

It was only in court that he discovered Uncle Harry had shopped him. To save him, the old man said. The memory of how he'd hated Uncle Harry for that betrayal came flooding back—as did the follow-up, which made him smile. The old man had sent him a computer—'courtesy of his conscience', the greeting card had said. Heath had left it unpacked in his cell until one day curiosity got the better of him—and the rest was history.

His stint inside had left him wiser. He could make money, but not with his fists. Uncle Harry's computer was the answer. On his release he set up an office in his bedroom where no one could see him or judge him, and no one knew how young he was, or how poor. All he had to do was click a mouse and the world came to him. And the world liked his games.

Heath moved on as the wall he'd been leaning against shuddered a complaint. He was stronger than he knew—which was more than could be said for the fabric of this place. One good shove and the whole lot would come tumbling down. It would be easier to flatten it and start again—

Since when had he embraced easy?

His fingers were already caressing the speed dial on his phone to call his architect when thoughts of plump pink lips and lush pert breasts intruded. Another pause, another memory—the last time he'd seen Bronte at Hebers Ghyll she'd been trying to save him from the police. She'd overheard Uncle Harry on the phone, and had run down the drive to warn him they were coming. When that had failed, she'd kissed him goodbye. He shook his head as he tried to blank the kiss. He'd better check she'd reached home safely.

He found Bronte still at the side of the road where she was having a bit of a disaster. The strap on her rucksack had given way and she was kneeling on the rolled-up groundsheet, lashing it into submission with a yard of rope and a clutch of nifty knots. Drawing the car to a halt, he leapt out. 'Wouldn't a regular buckle make things easier for you?'

'The buckles broke in Kathmandu.'

He curbed a grin. 'Of course they did.'

'No, really, they did,' she insisted, lifting her head. Then, remembering they weren't quite friends, she lowered it again, by which time her cheeks were glowing red.

'Want some help?' he offered.

'I can manage, thank you.'

'Play me a different tune, Bronte.' Having nudged her out of the way, he attached the rolled groundsheet to the top of her knapsack and started carrying it towards the car.

'We already know it won't fit in that ridiculous boot,' she yelled after him.

'Then I'll carry it home for you.'

'There's no need.' Racing up to him, she tried to pull it out of his hands.

'Do you want that interview or not?' he demanded, lifting it out of her reach.

'Does this mean you're keeping Hebers Ghyll?' she demanded, staring up at him.

'We'll see,' he said.

'Give.' She growled.

His lips curved as he looked down at her. 'Is that pleasant tone of voice supposed to entice me to hand it over?'

'Give, please,' she said with a scowl.

'Okay.' He helped her to hoist the rucksack onto her back again, careful not to let his fingers do any more work than strictly necessary.

Hefting the pack into a more comfortable position, she wobbled a little as she grew accustomed to the weight and then tottered off in the direction of home. He stayed close to make sure she was safe.

'I'm fine, Heath,' she called back to him over her shoulder, breaking into an unsteady jog.

'Watch out—the ground slopes away there—'

Too late. As Bronte stumbled on the treacherous bank he dived to save her. Catching his foot under a tree root, he took her with him, tumbling down the slope bound together as closely as two people could be.

'Bloody idiot!' she raged with shock as they thundered to a halt.

'Thank you would do it for me,' he observed mildly, noting the jagged rock he'd saved them from as well as the comfortable tangle of limbs.

'Thank you,' she huffed, snapping her hips away from his. 'The townie who thinks he can run Hebers Ghyll can't even keep his footing on a mossy bank,' she observed with biting relish.

'Is that dialect for welcome?' he said mildly.

'More like shove off.'

But she was in no hurry to move away. Lust. The desire to have, to possess, to inhabit, to pleasure and be pleasured sprang between them like a bright, hot flame. Bronte was shocked by the intensity of it. Her eyes blazed emerald fire into his and her lips had never been more kissable. She was aroused. And so was he.

Closing her eyes briefly, Bronte ground out a growl of impatience. She could of course slip back into her fantasy world and stay here wrapped around Heath—or she could get real and go home. 'Excuse me, please,' she said as politely as she could.

Heath yanked her to her feet. No courtesy involved. She let go of his hands. Fast—but not fast enough. Her body sang from his touch in three part harmony with baroque flourishes. She didn't argue this time when he offered to walk her home.

'Something funny?' Heath demanded when she looked at him and shook her head.

'The way you look?'

'That good?' He curved a smile.

'If camouflage is fashionable this season, you look great.'

'I heard mud, leaves and twigs are huge this year.' He brushed himself down.

She laughed. She couldn't help herself—just as she couldn't stop herself following Heath's hands jealously with her eyes. They were almost communicating again, Bronte realised—and that was dangerous. This was getting too much like the old days when her heart had been full of Heath.

So she'd hide how she felt about him—what was so hard about that?

They walked along in silence until Heath lobbed a curving ball. 'If I decide to keep the estate and call interviews, are you ready?'

'If you're serious, Heath, I'm ready now,' she exclaimed. 'That is if the new estate manager isn't just part of some lick of paint project to tart the place up so you can maximise your profit and get rid of it faster,' she added as common sense kicked in.

'Since when has profit been a dirty word?' Heath demanded.

'People are more important.'

'Which is why I'm the businessman and you're the dreamer, Bronte. Without profit there can be no jobs—no people living in Hebers Ghyll. And I won't be rushed into this. I never make a decision until I know all the facts.'

'Then know this,' she said as their exchange heated up. 'You and I could never work in any sort of team.'

'No,' Heath agreed. 'I'd always be the boss.'

'You're unbelievable.'

'So they tell me.'

With an incredulous laugh Bronte tossed her burnished mane and quickened her step to get ahead of him. He kept up easily. 'If I do decide to do anything it won't be half-hearted. It will be all about renewal and regeneration.'

'Sounds impressive,' she said. 'Almost unbelievable.'

Bronte had always scored a gold star for sarcasm. She was paying him back for doubting her. And why was he even discussing something that was barely a glimmer of an idea? 'My hobby's building things—I've carried out restoration work in the past so I know what's involved.' And now defending it?

He got what he deserved.

'Get real, Heath,' Bronte flashed. 'This isn't cyberspace. You can't conjure up an idyllic country scene on your screen complete with a fully restored castle, click your mouse and wipe out years of under-investment.'

'No, but I can try. I might not be the countryside's biggest fan, but I'm not known for running out.'

'And neither am I,' she shot back.

'Are we agreed on something?'

She huffed.

'The only way Hebers Ghyll can survive is for people like you to get involved, Bronte.'

'Oh, I see,' she said. 'People like me do all the hard work while you direct us from your city desk? Unless you're going to live here, Heath, which I doubt.'

'Do you want Hebers Ghyll to have a future or not? Yes or no, Bronte? If you're serious about trying to get people to come back here there has to be something for them to come back to.'

'So now you're a visionary?'

'No. I'm a realist.' And he liked a challenge—especially when there was a woman involved.

'This is nothing like the city, Heath.'

'Isn't it?' he fired back. 'The air might be polluted with pollen instead of smoke, but, like you said, jobs are just as hard to find. So you go right ahead and walk away, Bronte. Let Hebers Ghyll slide into a hole. Or you can stay and fight.'

'With you? What changed your mind, Heath?'

Heath's face closed off. Why didn't she know when to keep quiet? She could only guess how he must have felt coming back here. She returned to the fray to divert him. 'You can't just plonk down a couple of computers in the village hall, maintain a cyber presence and think that's enough, Heath. People need proper work—and a proper leader on site to direct them.'

'Are you saying you wouldn't be up to that?'

'I'd do whatever was expected of me, and more, if I were lucky enough to get the job,' Bronte countered, rejoicing in Heath's attack. The way he was talking could only mean he was seriously interested in keeping the estate.

'Judging by your enthusiasm you'd work happily alongside anyone who does get the job?'

He'd got her. Damn it. Heath had always been a master tactician. She threw him a thunderous look.

He was all logic while Bronte was the flip side of the coin—all that passion with so little curb on it made it so easy to outmanoeuvre her, it was hardly fair. He hadn't made a final decision yet. The problems at Hebers Ghyll were nothing new for him. There had been no work in his old neighbourhood, but he had known that if there was enough money for tools and equipment there would be more than enough jobs for everyone. 'There's only one problem,' he said, reeling her in.

'Which is?' she demanded on cue.

'You.' He stared directly at her. 'You're the problem, Bronte. If I consider you for the job I have to bear in mind you took off once and went travelling. How do I know you won't do that again?'

'Because my travels had a purpose and now I'm home to put what I've learned into practice.'

'That's good,' he agreed, 'but if I take this on there will be nothing but hard work ahead, and a lot of difficult decisions to be made. I need to be sure that whoever I employ as estate manager has both the staying power and the backbone for what needs to be done.'

'What are you implying, Heath?'

He lifted the latch on the wooden gate that led through to her parents' garden. 'I'm saying I don't know you, Bronte. I only know what you're telling me. It's been a long time.'

'For both of us,' she reminded him tensely.

He propped her rucksack against the front door.

'Hey,' she said when he turned to leave. 'Where are you going? We're in the middle of a conversation.'

'We'll continue it another time. I have to get back now.'

'Can't we talk first? What's the hurry?'

Strangely, it pleased him that she wanted to keep him back. 'I have appointments I can't break. My work is in London, remember? It's where I make the money that might just keep this place alive.' He stopped at the gate and turned to face her. 'Just promise me one thing before I go.'

'What?'

'Parts of Hebers Ghyll aren't safe, Bronte, so please stay away.'

'The Great Hall's safe,' she insisted stubbornly. 'Uncle Harry was living there up to a few months ago.'

'And I'm telling you not to go near it until I get back.'

'So you are coming back?'

As her eyes fired he propped a hip against the garden wall. 'You'll be telling me how much you'll miss me next.'

'Ha! Don't hold your breath.'

'If you need me you've got my number.'

'What use is that when your PA won't put me through?'

'You give up too easily, Bronte.' Raising his hand in a farewell salute, he thought himself lucky to be out of range of any missiles she might have to hand.

CHAPTER FOUR

WHEN Heath left her Bronte was still high on adrenalin hours later. She needed action. Lots of it. She went back to Hebers Ghyll and broke in. Maybe this was the craziest idea she'd had yet, but she wasn't prepared to be run off a property she had always thought of as her second home. The moment Heath's car roared away she made some calls to girls in the village—girls who'd been friends for life. The chance to do a little exploring was right up their street.

How dangerous could the Great Hall be? It had only stood empty for a couple of months. She wouldn't take any chances, Bronte determined as she led her troops beneath a moody sky down the long overgrown drive. Everyone knew the castle was ready to fall down, but the hall where her mother had been housekeeper, and the rooms where Uncle Harry had used to live, they were safe. Heath was overreacting—or, more likely, trying to keep her away. She had explained to her friends, Maisie and Colleen, that there were no-go areas and that they mustn't go off exploring on their own.

'This is spooky,' Colleen said, echoing Bronte's thoughts as they all flashed an anxious glance into the impenetrable undergrowth.

They could speed-walk to international standards by

the time they reached the open space where a dried-up moat circled the ruined castle. The castle was a heap of blackened stone, lowering and forbidding beneath boiling storm clouds, and the ugly gash around it was full of brambles and leaves. 'Nice,' Colleen murmured.

It needed clearing—needed filling—needed ducks, Bronte thought. She wouldn't have trusted the drawbridge—most of the planks were missing, and a glance at the rusty portcullis hanging over it confirmed that Heath was right to warn her to stay away. But even the old castle could be transformed like one she'd seen in France. The fortress of Carcassonne had been faithfully restored and was now a World Heritage site. But that was for another day. 'We'll go straight to the Great Hall,' she told the girls, leading them swiftly past the danger zone.

Excitement started to bubble inside Bronte the moment she stood in front of the old hall. The sun had made a welcome return, burning through the clouds, and the warmth and light changed everything. It raised her spirits and softened the blackened stone, turning it rosy. This could all be so romantic, if it weren't so run-down. Her plan had been to bring the girls along to enthuse them, but she clearly had a long way to go. They had gone quiet, which was a bad sign. 'Come on,' she said in an attempt to lift their spirits. 'Let's see what we've got round the back.'

More decay. Dried-up fountains. Tangled weeds. Crumbling stone.

For a moment she felt overwhelmed, defeated, but then she determined that she would find a way. Scrambling through an upstairs window, she brushed herself down. The echoing landing smelled musty and dust hung like a curtain in the shadowy air. She could hardly expect

Heath to feel enthusiastic about this, Bronte mused as she walked slowly down the stairs, let alone spend his hard-earned money putting it right.

She could only hope the girls would stick with her, Bronte concluded as she picked her way across the broken floor tiles in the hall. How depressing to see how quickly everything had deteriorated. It didn't help to know she had only added to the destruction. She'd tried her mother's door key, only to discover that the one useful thing the previous estate manager had done before Heath sacked him was to change the locks. Adapting her plans accordingly, she had shinned up a drainpipe, forced a window and climbed in. And this was not the testimony to Uncle Harry's generosity that he deserved. Plants had withered and died, while chairs had mysteriously fallen over, and plaster was falling off the walls faster than the mice could eat it.

Shouldn't Heath be here doing something about this?

And why was she thinking about Heath when she could just as easily do something about it? She had already established that Heath's interest in his inheritance was mild at most. Heath only cared about the profit he could make when he sold it on. He'd made that clear enough. He could barely spare the time for this weekend's flying visit. Heath's life was all about making money in London now.

With a frustrated growl, she scraped her hair back into a band ready for work—only to be rewarded by an image of Heath in her mind, standing beneath the vaulted ceiling of the Great Hall looking like a conquering hero as he fixed her with his mocking stare.

Why did it always have to come back to Heath?

Because Heath was blessed with such an overdose of

darkly brooding charisma it was impossible not to think about him, Bronte concluded. But a man like Heath could hardly be expected to hang around when there were so many people waiting to admire him—and she was hardly the swooning type. So, who needed him? There was nothing here she couldn't handle.

Having convinced herself that she had ejected Heath from her thoughts, she now had to confront all the other impressions crowding in. 'I'm going to change this,' she murmured, staring round.

'Talking to yourself, Lady Muck?' Colleen called down to her from the upstairs landing.

Bronte's heart leapt. So the girls had decided to join her. 'You made it,' she called back. 'Come and join me. We've got the place to ourselves.'

'No boarders to repel?' Maisie demanded, sounding disappointed as she clattered down the stairs in a cloud of cheap scent and good humour. 'I thought there'd be at least one hunky ghost for me to deal with.'

Or Heath in full battle armour with a demolition ball at his command, Bronte mused—that was one boarder she wouldn't have minded repelling. Or, better still— half-naked Heath, muscles bulging, on his knees in front of her. Much better. She'd keep that one—as well as the quiver of awareness that accompanied it. Enough! she told herself firmly as a puff of plaster dust landed on her shoulder. Heath had gone back to London, and there was work to be done here. 'There should be life at Hebers Ghyll,' she announced to the girls. 'We can't let it crumble to dust and do nothing about it.'

'Aye aye, Captain.'

The girls delivered a mock-salute as Bronte warmed to her theme. 'There should be life and warmth and music—and there will be again.'

The girls whooped and cheered. 'How about we help you after work and at weekends?' Colleen suggested when they'd all calmed down.

Bronte was moved by the offer. 'I couldn't ask you to do that.'

'Why not?' Maisie demanded. 'It could be fun.'

'Spiders are fun?' Bronte seemed doubtful.

'Well, we can't leave you here on your own, can we?' Colleen pointed out. 'If you're going to be battling ghosts and spiders, we want to be part of it, don't we, Maisie?'

'I'll trade you my most excellent work with a broom and a ghost-busters kit, for a drink at the pub,' Maisie suggested. 'How about that?'

'Deal,' Bronte agreed. 'Let's get to it,' she announced, leading the way to the storeroom where the cleaning equipment was kept.

'Working party present and correct,' Colleen confirmed once they were armed with brushes and bin liners. 'Where would you like us to start?'

'Not with mouse droppings or spiders' webs,' Maisie protested, wielding her dustpan. 'The only thing I'm prepared to scream for is a man.'

I wish, Bronte thought, imagining she was in a clinch with Heath. 'The best I can offer you is a good scrumping in the apple orchard.'

'I think Maisie had something more hands on in mind than that,' Colleen suggested dryly.

'You do surprise me. Why don't we clear up as much as we can in here and then reward ourselves with a swim in the lake?'

'Skinny-dipping?' Her friends shrieked, hugging themselves in anticipation.

'Well, as we haven't moved in with our fourteen

wardrobes of clothes yet—seems skinny-dipping is our only option.'

'Could you arrange for the lake to be heated before we dive in?' Colleen demanded.

'You'll soon get warm,' Bronte promised as visions of childhood's endless summer days spent swimming or rowing on the lake filled her head with slightly rose-tinted images—swiftly followed by red-hot thoughts of Heath rising like a wet-shirted Mr Darcy dripping water from his muscular frame—

'Bronte?' the girls prompted.

'Sorry.' Tearing her thoughts away from Heath, Bronte focused on the here and now. It would be lonely at the hall without the girls and working together promised to be fun.

And if Heath never came back?

They'd get by somehow. But because she was stubborn she was going to make that call to London to check if he would be holding interviews for jobs at the hall.

'Daydreaming about Heath *again*?' Colleen teased her.

'I've got bigger things on my mind than Heath,' Bronte replied, trying to look serious.

'Bigger than Heath?' Colleen exclaimed, exchanging a knowing look with Maisie.

'You're disgusting.' Bronte smothered a smile.

The business trip he had left Hebers Ghyll to make had been a resounding success. He was back in town within the week, brooding in his office with Bronte on his mind. She was too inquisitive to quietly settle back into life at the cottage, which worried him. She wouldn't be able to resist taking another look round Hebers Ghyll, which was dangerous. She could be down there now with a bundle of energy and good intentions. He'd made sure everything was locked up securely before he left, but he didn't trust her—and good intentions wouldn't stop those walls falling on her head. He had no option. He had to go back.

He called Quentin from the car to make arrangements to cover his absence at the board meeting, and then he made a few more calls. There was no point in his going to Hebers Ghyll on a day trip—or just to yell at Bronte. He might as well start moving things forward. Whether or not he decided to keep the estate it could only benefit from a refit. And he could only benefit either way.

The two girls were as good as their word and came to the hall every night after work to help Bronte sort things out. One week of back-breaking work was nearly over and there was still no sign of Heath.

Still no answer on his phone either. Perhaps he'd given her the wrong number on purpose—or perhaps Heath's PA was even more efficient than she'd thought him, which was entirely possible. She couldn't pretend she wasn't disappointed that Heath had just disappeared again as if that visit had never happened, but she hid her feelings from the girls, and stubbornly refused to let it get her down. She distracted herself by working as hard as she could until all she could think about at night was a soft pillow and a long, dreamless sleep.

By the end of the week the three girls had systematically cleared, cleaned, and de-spidered the Great Hall, and had returned the kitchen to its former pristine state. They had weeded the formal gardens as well as the kitchen garden with its wealth of vegetables, and cheered when Bronte, whose hands and face seemed to be permanently covered in sticky black oil for most of the time, finally managed to get the sit-on lawnmower to work. Having tamed the grass and cleared the rubbish, a small part of the Hebers Ghyll estate, if not exactly restored to its former glory, was at least clean and tidy, and as a bonus they were all suntanned and healthy thanks to a timely Indian summer. And they were definitely well fed, thanks to Bronte's frequent raids on the vegetable patch. There was only one fly in this late-summer ointment as far as Bronte was concerned, and that was Heath. You'd think he'd want to know the place was still standing…

One hazy late afternoon when even the bees could hardly be bothered to hum, Bronte was down at the lakeside with Colleen and Maisie.

'What are you doing?' Colleen demanded grumpily when Bronte reached for her phone. 'You can't be ringing *him* again?'

'Yes, *him* again,' Bronte confirmed, firming her jaw. 'Heath gave me this number, and some time or other I'm bound to get through to him.'

'Dreamer,' Maisie commented.

'When he takes his phone off call divert,' Colleen added.

'Well, I'm not going to give up.'

'What a surprise,' Maisie murmured, brushing a harmless hover-fly away.

The phone droned. Bronte waited. And then sprang to attention. But it was only Heath's PA, who put her off in the same weary tone. Colleen and Maisie were right. Heath had no intention of speaking to her ever again.

'When are you going to get it through your head—' Colleen began as Bronte snapped the phone shut and tossed it on the ground.

'Don't,' she said. 'Just…don't.'

Bronte's friends fell silent as she flung herself down on the grass. Lying flat on her back, she gazed up through a lace of leaves to the hint of blue sky beyond. What if Heath sold the estate? What if he'd already sold it and they were all ejected? She should spare the girls that. They could be arrested. This was so unfair. They were seeing progress. They had a routine going. And a goal—Christmas in the Great Hall, recreating one of Uncle Harry's famous Christmas parties. Bronte imagined inviting everyone in the village. How could she disappoint Colleen and Maisie now when they'd worked so hard to achieve that?

What Heath might think about them planning a Christmas party without his say-so was something she would think about another day.

'The lake's too cold for swimming,' Colleen announced, distracting Bronte from her thoughts. 'I'm going home. Are you coming, Bronte?'

Maisie was on her feet too.

'No, you go on,' Bronte said. 'I'm going to have a quick swim.'

Pulling off her clothes as the girls disappeared through the trees, she stretched her naked body in the sun. Before she had chance to chicken out she scampered to the edge of the lake and plunged in. The shock of the icy water sucked all the breath out of her. She flailed around for a moment before steadying and starting to swim. Powering out to the centre of the lake with a relaxed, easy stroke, she turned on her back and floated blissfully in the silence...

Silence?

What silence?

Shooting up, she turned her head, trying to locate the source of a steady rumbling noise. It sounded like an armoured tank division coming down the drive. She swung around in the water, trying to work out how she could claim her clothes before anyone saw her—

Forget it, Bronte concluded as the rumbling grew louder. She'd never make it in time. She would just have to stay here, treading water...

Where was she? Heath frowned as he peered through the windscreen. Bronte was his first—his only thought as he drove up the drive. He'd called in at the cottage. She wasn't there. The old lady next door said Bronte would be up at Hebers Ghyll—as if it was a regular thing. He'd been angry since that moment—concerned and furious that Bronte had ignored everything he'd told her. But still, he'd hoped to see a flash of purple leggings—a glint of sun-kissed hair. Instead, all he could see were two other girls, sauntering out of the woods at the side of the lake as if they owned the place. So where the hell was she? And what the hell was going on?

Swinging down from the cab of his utility vehicle, he waited for the other men to assemble. Having issued preliminary instructions, he strode towards the girls. He wasn't interested in entering into conversation with them. He wanted the answer to one simple question: 'Where's Bronte?' he demanded, addressing the bleached blonde with a confident air.

'Heath Stamp,' she murmured. 'Is it really you?'

'I need to see her,' he said, ignoring the girl's attempt to distract him.

'I'm Colleen,' the girl persisted. 'Don't you remember me? And this is Maisie—'

'Where is she?' he cut across her in an ominous growl.

'A real charmer,' Colleen murmured.

'So what's changed?' Maisie agreed beneath her breath.

Both girls were staring at him warily now. So they remembered him. 'Are you going to tell me where she is?'

'I-in the lake,' Maisie stammered.

'In the lake?' he said, swinging round.

'Swimming,' Colleen hurried to explain.

As he turned to look he saw something that had him storming across the lawn, tugging off his clothes as he ran.

CHAPTER FIVE

SHE'D got trapped in the weeds. She'd been so trauma-
tised by the truck invasion she'd blundered about in the
water wondering what to do next and had got her leg
caught. Throwing her arms around as she struggled to
free herself, Bronte had attracted the very type of attention she had been trying to avoid. The long line of
wagons and builders' vans, led by a rugged Jeep with
blacked-out windows, had parked up in front of the hall.
Her heart jolted painfully to see Heath spring down
from the lead vehicle. Having spoken to the girls, he
turned to look at the lake at the precise moment she
started thrashing about. Impossibly bronzed and muscular, Heath, having tossed his shirt away as he ran,
was clearly intent on launching a one-man rescue. The
only option left to her was to swim as fast as she could
in the opposite direction.

Forget it, Bronte concluded, treading water. Her best
effort wasn't nearly good enough. Heath was streaking
towards her with a strong, fast stroke and had soon cut
off her escape route. Before she had chance to change
direction he gathered her up like a rugby ball and kicked
for shore.

'Put me down!' she shrieked the instant Heath found

his feet and started wading. 'I'm warning you, Heath—let me go. There's no need for this.'

'There's every need for this.' Heath sounded less than amused. Dumping her on her feet on the middle of the lawn, he stood back.

She had never seen anyone quite so furious. She hunched over, acutely conscious of her nakedness.

Heath seemed disappointingly unaware of it. 'What did I tell you before I left?' he demanded.

Bronte's face flushed red. 'I haven't been near the old buildings—'

'So you swim in the lake on your own? Brilliant.'

Heath's expression was thunderous. All male. All disapproval. And the sight of his naked torso—powerful beyond belief, wet, tanned and gleaming in the sun—was an unnerving distraction. She jumped alert the moment she realised Heath's narrowed gaze was roving freely over her naked body as if it were his to inspect. 'Do you mind?' she flared, covering herself as best she could.

'What the hell did you think you were doing in the lake?' Heath snapped as if they were both fully clothed.

'Swimming,' she said as if that were obvious. 'And I know what I'm doing.'

Heath took one look at her. 'That would be a first.'

'Can't you turn your back or something?'

He ignored this remark. 'Never swim in the lake again on your own. Do you understand me?'

'Perfectly.' She was trying to edge towards her clothes, which wasn't easy with her legs crossed. At last she managed to snag her leggings with the thong still tangled inside them. Snatching them up with relief, she held them in front of her. However ridiculous she looked, it was some sort of shield. All she could do now was to start moving backwards, away from him.

She should have seen the tree root coming. She should have known that lightning did sometimes strike the same place twice. The breath flew from her lungs as Heath dived to save her—by some miracle he managed to swing her around before she hit the ground, cushioning her fall with his body. She was too shocked by the impact to do anything but yell, 'Get off me!' And scowl down.

Heath grinned up. 'I think you would have to get off me,' he pointed out.

Oh, great. She was straddling him, and Heath was clearly enjoying every moment of it—as well he might, with his great big hands firmly attached to her backside. 'Let me go,' she insisted, wriggling furiously. But the moment Heath lifted his hands away she missed them and wanted them back again. Fortunately for her, common sense kicked in.

'You don't really want to do that, do you, Bronte?'

She turned to look back over her shoulder at Heath.

'Seriously, it's not your best look,' he assured her as she continued to crawl away.

All she cared about was reaching a covey of trees over to her left where there were bushes to hide in while she sorted out her clothes. 'What do you think you're doing?' she shrieked with surprise.

Heath had grabbed her and trapped her beneath him on the ground. 'Preserving your dignity,' he said calmly, 'or what little remains of it.'

She followed his gaze. And groaned. Maisie, Colleen, and all of Heath's men had gathered at a safe distance to watch their little drama play out.

'Don't say it,' Heath warned her in a low growl. 'I can't bear to hear a woman swear.'

'Swear? I can barely draw enough breath to speak with you on top of me. Well—get up,' she insisted, only to be rewarded by a wolfish grin. 'Get off me, please,' she said reluctantly as their audience scattered. 'We weren't expecting visitors,' she said, acutely conscious of her naked body pressed into Heath's naked chest.

'Clearly,' he murmured, gazing down at her.

He seemed in no hurry to move away. 'Why didn't you warn me you were coming?' she said, thinking it best to make conversation in a position like this.

'Warn a squatter the owner's on his way?'

'I'm not a squatter,' Bronte argued. Her gaze slipped from Heath's mocking eyes to his sexy mouth, where it lingered. 'We're not even staying at the hall,' she protested faintly.

'And I should be grateful for that?'

She should be grateful for this, Bronte reflected, telling herself to relax and enjoy—would this moment ever come again?

'When will you get it through your head that Hebers Ghyll is not yours to do with as you like, Bronte?'

Nor was Heath's magnificent body, unfortunately. 'We were only trying to help.'

'Against my express instructions.'

'We stayed away from the castle.'

'Next time, do me the courtesy of asking if you can visit my property first. This obviously comes as a surprise to you, but this is my land, and safety is an overriding concern of mine.'

How could it be when Heath's chest hair was tormenting her nipples? The men she met on her travels were too busy fretting about their skin care regime or whether or not to wax their chest. Heath clearly suffered no such dilemmas.

'Well, this is nice,' he remarked, easing his position, which made her blink. 'I never took you for a nudist, Bronte.'

'And I never took you for Genghis Khan,' she fired back in an attempt to blank the sensation currently flooding her veins.

'Oh, yes, you did,' Heath growled softly.

Was it safer to stare into his eyes and see what he was thinking, or at Heath's firm mouth and long to kiss him? She was in trouble whatever she did, Bronte concluded, while Heath was hot-wired to all her erotic pressure points. She took the only option left open to her, and closed her eyes, shutting him out.

'Open your eyes, Bronte. This is no time to fall asleep.'

Or to experience that first seductive brush of Heath's lips, apparently. 'Oh, clear off,' she flared, trying to push him away. 'What are you made of?' she demanded when he didn't yield. 'Kryptonite?'

'Flesh and blood the same as you.'

'Not a bit like me,' Bronte argued primly.' I have manners.'

'And a naked bottom,' Heath commented mildly as she struggled to cover herself with an impossibly shrunken pair of leggings.

'You're such a barbarian.'

'Come on—get dressed.' As Heath sprang up he dragged her with him. 'This has gone on long enough, Bronte. You're still a trespasser with a lot of explaining to do.'

Snatching her hands free, she was crouched down in a ball again. 'Later,' she said. 'You can leave me now.'

'Oh, can I?' Heath demanded, planting his hands on his hips.

'Honestly,' she flared—though flaring was difficult from a crouching position. 'I really can't believe your ingratitude. We cleared *your* house—*your* grounds—'

'And if a wall had fallen on *your* head?'

'I already told you, we haven't been anywhere dangerous.'

'You've been back to the hall,' said Heath, who showed no sign of going anywhere.

'Do you seriously think I'd take the girls into a dangerous situation?'

'No, but you'd walk blindly in,' Heath argued. 'And you'd probably be hit by falling masonry before you got halfway through the door.'

'There's no need to sound quite so thrilled by the prospect.'

'Leaving me to clear up the mess,' he finished, talking over her. 'When I say don't do something, there's a very good reason for it.'

Oh, why wouldn't her clothes co-operate on damp skin? Her leggings had twisted round like a self-imposed chastity belt. All she could do was crunch over with her arms covering her chest as Heath threw her her top.

'When were you going to tell me about the window, Bronte?'

She froze mid-pulling it on.

'What?' Heath barked. 'You thought I wouldn't notice?'

She hadn't meant to do it and felt terrible. When she had forced the upstairs window to break into the hall the handle had come away in her hand. 'Oh, Heath, I'm really sorry—'

'Are you?' he said impassively. His hands on his hips, he confronted her with a stony gaze.

Displaying a truly magnificent chest, Bronte registered with a sharp intake of breath. She had forgotten how tall Heath was, how impossibly fit. And with nothing to cover those massive blacksmith's arms, or his powerful torso—

'Have you done staring?' he snapped.

'I'm going home,' Bronte announced in exasperation. 'I need to wash this mud off.'

'I'd say be my guest,' Heath observed sardonically, 'but as you have already made yourself at home.'

'I prefer to use my own shower, thank you,' she snapped back.

'As you wish.'

But now Heath stood in her way. Feinting past him, she snatched up the last of her clothes. 'I don't need anything from you, Heath.'

'Except a job, presumably?'

She froze.

'You're not going the right way about it, are you?' Heath pointed out. 'You broke into my house. You brought your friends along too.'

'This has nothing to do with Maisie or Colleen,' Bronte interrupted, rushing to her friends' defence. 'This is all my fault, Heath. Blame me, if you must. I was just trying to help. I thought that if we.'

'You didn't think,' Heath interrupted her sharply. 'You went straight into an old building without a safety review—just as you swam solo in the lake. I could forgive that, but you got your friends involved and that was irresponsible. Or had you conveniently forgotten that breaking and entering is a criminal offence? Go home, Bronte,' he rapped when she tried to defend her decision. 'I can't believe you're serious about applying for a job here. If that's still the case, you've made one hell of a start. I can't imagine how you're going to climb back from this.'

And neither could she. Heath's tone of voice made it clear that playtime was well and truly over.

She had alienated Heath. She had forfeited her chance of getting the job. She had lost the girls their promised pay-off—the Christmas party—which meant that all their hard work was wasted.

Things couldn't be worse, Bronte mused back at the cottage, where she was sitting on the sofa with her head buried in her hands.

So she'd just have to make it right, she determined, springing to her feet.

Heath couldn't possibly have appeared less thrilled when she turned up at the hall with Colleen and Maisie in tow.

'What do you want, Bronte?' he rapped, while she stood and stared. Heath in hard hat, steel-capped boots, and a high-vis' jacket, was a fantasy yet to be explored.

'We're here to help,' she said, conscious of Maisie and Colleen skulking behind her. The girls hadn't been exactly enthusiastic when she had sold them this idea over a drink at the pub.

'Help?' Heath demanded, narrowing his eyes suspiciously. 'We're on the roof, Bronte. How can you help?'

'Has the fresh air given you an appetite, possibly?' she enquired pleasantly.

'Why? Did you bring pizza?' Heath looked behind her to see if the girls were carrying anything.

'No.' Bronte shook her head. 'I'd only serve pizza if I'd made it myself. I was merely suggesting I could cook supper for you—but if you'd rather we left—'

'You cook?' Heath interrupted.

'Of course I cook. My mother was the housekeeper here,' she reminded him with a frown. 'And as you pointed out,' she added innocently, 'I have a great line in jam tarts. But don't stereotype me. I mend engines too.'

Heath hummed. 'I suppose the men will need feeding when they knock off, so if you're offering to cook supper for nine—'

'Twelve,' Bronte said, turning to look at the girls. 'I'll get started, shall I?'

With some reluctance, it seemed to Bronte, Heath stepped aside. The way to a man's heart would always be by the same route—something women knew and had used shamelessly across the ages. She was hardly a trailblazer in that regard, Bronte reflected as she led her troops towards the kitchen.

CHAPTER SIX

SUPPER was nearly ready. They just needed some fresh herbs for the soup, which Colleen and Maisie had offered to go and pick for her while Bronte kept an eye on things on the cooker. It was Colleen who drew Bronte's attention to the tableau being played out in the yard outside the kitchen window.

There was no harm in looking, was there? She joined her friends on the pretext of opening the window to let the steam out from her soup.

Heath, dressed just in jeans, was sluicing down in the yard.

Oh, yes, he was…

And very nice he looked too…

As he slowly tipped a bucket of water from the well over his head drops of water glittered in the last rays of the sun and flew from his hair as he raked it back with big, rough hands. She felt rather than heard him sigh with pleasure. And then those hands continued on as Heath slid the last of the water from his hard-muscled chest…

'Oh, my God—you could have an orgasm just watching him,' Colleen breathed, leaning over Bronte's shoulder.

'Shh! He'll hear us.' Bronte held her breath.

'I didn't even know men came built like that,' Maisie confided.

'They don't,' Colleen assured her. 'You want to get stuck in there, Bronte.'

'Me?' Bronte pretended innocence as she pressed a hand against her chest. 'Heath isn't interested in me.'

'Not much,' Colleen murmured, still avidly watching.

'Well, even if he was—'

'He is,' Colleen assured her with the resulting impact on Bronte's pulse.

'Well, let's get on,' she said, sounding rather like her mother, Bronte thought.

Inwardly, she was anything but. Her mother was calm and logical, while Bronte was a dreamer on a roller-coaster ride out of control. Her heart refused to stop thumping as Colleen and Maisie, having put Heath out of their minds, started laying up the long, scrubbed table. Then another horrible thought occurred—if her fantasies were an open book to her friends, they must be clear to Heath as well!

'Why wouldn't you be interested in a man like that?' Colleen demanded, doggedly returning to the subject as she came back for the spoons. 'You haven't been putting bromide in your tea, have you, Bronte?'

'Just sugar,' Bronte murmured distractedly, jumping back from the window too late to stop Heath seeing her.

Holding onto Bronte's shoulders so she could stare over them, Colleen observed, 'Licking that chunky-hunk is all the sugar I'd ever need.'

'Supper's in ten,' Bronte pointed out briskly, 'and I need those herbs before I serve up.'

'On it,' Colleen promised. Grabbing Maisie by

the wrist, she left Bronte to her own devices in the kitchen.

Heath came into the room moments later. He grunted. She grunted. She didn't trust herself to turn around. She could hear him moving around behind her—hanging up his jacket, putting his hard hat on the side, taking off his boots and leaving them on the mat by the door.

Had her senses ever been this keen before?

Warm man…a little ruffled, a little windswept, his hair a little damp—his jeans definitely wet, and clinging lovingly—

'Hey, what do you think you're doing?' she said, jumping with alarm as Heath brushed past her.

'Stealing soup,' he said. 'It smelled so good—'

'Hands off,' she said, smacking his hand away. 'And there's no need to sound so surprised.'

Heath's expression was deceptively sleepy, Bronte thought, with his face so close, and his eyes… 'Must you creep up on me?' Must you look so sexy? she thought, taking in the damply dangerous man who looked exactly like the answer to her every sex-starved dream.

'I didn't creep.' The sexy mouth tugged up in a grin. 'I think you'll find on closer acquaintance that I never creep.'

No, he never did, and that sluice-down in the yard had really intensified the scent of warm, clean man. And what did he mean by closer acquaintance? As she tried to work it out she dragged in greedy lungfuls of Heath's delicious scent when what she should be doing was watching the food on top of the cooker to make sure it didn't burn.

Her gaze started at ground level with Heath's sexy feet, and then rose steadily to take in the hard thighs stretching the seams on his damp jeans. She resolutely refused to notice the button open at the top of his zipper, or the belt hanging loose—and moved on swiftly to Heath's impressive chest, which was currently clad in the deep blue heavy-knit sweater he'd pulled on at the door—

She yelped with shock when he took hold of her elbows and lifted her aside. Heath shrugged. 'I'd hate you to burn that soup. And I owe it to the men to make sure you know what you're doing,' he added, stealing another spoonful. 'What?' he said, angling his chin as Bronte planted her hands on her hips. 'You didn't think I'd give you a completely free rein, did you?'

'You don't frighten me, Heath Stamp. Now, get out of my way—'

'Not before I've had another spoonful. This soup isn't bad,' Heath admitted. His amused glance made Bronte wonder if he was remembering her naked.

'If you want to catch your death in those wet jeans go right ahead,' she said.

'They're not drying as I'd hoped,' Heath said, his lips pressing down. 'Why don't you sling them over the Aga rail for me?'

'Like I want your wet clothes hanging in my kitchen? And don't even think of lounging round in your boxers while I'm making a meal.'

'You're making two assumptions there,' Heath told her, 'both of which are wrong.'

One: it wasn't her kitchen, it was Heath's.

And two?

Don't even go there, Bronte thought, noting the humour in Heath's eyes. 'I was merely suggesting you might want to change into some dry clothes before supper,' she told him primly.

'And if I had some dry clothes with me, I might do that.'

Heath had lightened up. Maybe breaks in the country were good for him, Bronte reasoned. Pity they weren't good for her composure.

And while she was musing on this Heath stole some more soup from the pot. 'There'll be none left,' she protested spreading out her arms to take command of the Aga. 'Here,' she said, opening the oven door. 'Why don't you stick your butt in there? You'll soon dry off.'

'That's a little drastic, isn't it?' Heath observed.

'It's an accepted method of warming up.'

'Really?' Heath said, making her wish she hadn't spoken. Folding her arms, she angled her chin as she waited for him to take her advice.

'Thank you, but no,' he said, allowing her a small mocking bow. 'I'm sure my body heat will take care of it.'

It was certainly taking care of her.

'Do I make you nervous, Bronte?'

'As if,' she scoffed. 'Though you do make me a bit nervous,' she said on reflection.

'Oh?' Heath's gaze flared with interest.

'You're eating all the soup,' she told him deadpan. 'Now clear off—'

She exhaled sharply as Heath caught hold of her arm as he brushed past. 'Why did you really come back to the hall, Bronte?'

'Why did you come back?' she said, feeling unusually flustered as she stared up at him.

'I asked you first.'

'I took pity on you—and, okay, I made a fuss about you doing something with your inheritance. I could hardly sit at home twiddling my thumbs after that.'

'To think, I almost drove you away,' Heath said, heaving a heavy sigh. 'Where did I go wrong?'

'I don't know, Heath.' She met the humorous gaze head on—and wished she hadn't. Hadn't she made enough mistakes for one day?

'Let me repeat myself,' Heath said, 'What are you really doing here, Bronte?'

'I couldn't stay away from you,' she said in her most mocking tone. 'Does that make you feel better?'

'At least you're being honest,' Heath said.

'You're so modest,' Bronte countered, stirring the soup as if her life depended on it. 'You know my only interest in being here is the future of Hebers Ghyll.'

'Liar,' Heath said softly.

'Could you put these bowls out for me, please?' She plonked them in his hands. Anything to keep Heath's hands occupied and give herself space to think.

'I have made you feel better, haven't I?' Heath sounded pleased with himself as he came back to prop a hip against the side.

'So good I hardly know what to do with myself,' Bronte agreed, sticking the salt pot and pepper grinder in his hands. 'Now move. You definitely can't stand this close to the heat without—'

'Without both of us getting burned?' Heath suggested.

'Without the soup getting burned,' she corrected him. 'Excuse me please…' Would her heart stop thundering? Hands on hips, she waited for Heath to move. Her only alternative was to stretch across him—and risk rubbing some already highly aroused and very sensitive part of her body against him? Not even remotely sensible to try.

'I'm still wondering what you came back for,' he said, 'and I mean the real reason.'

'Okay,' she said, staring him in the eyes. 'I'm serious about wanting the job and I thought if I came here and made myself useful—doing anything I could to help— you might remember me when it came to handing out interview times.'

Leaning back against the Aga rail, Heath crossed his arms and gave her one of his looks. 'So you're here so you can keep on reminding me how good you'd be?'

That wasn't quite the way she would have put it, but yes. 'I thought cooking supper for you would be a start.'

'And you're not a conniving woman?'

Heath's face was very close—close enough to see how thick his lashes were, and how firm his mouth. 'On the contrary,' Bronte argued, 'I am a conniving woman. And I know what I want.'

'And so do I,' Heath assured her as he straightened up.

'Well, seeing as you've shown willing.'

Heath laughed.

And now he was standing in her way again. 'Excuse me, please,' she said politely.

What was she supposed to do with a man who took up every inch of vital cooking space and who showed no sign of moving—a man who was staring down at her now with a look in his darkening eyes that suggested he would very much like a practical demonstration of just how badly she wanted to work for him? 'You're in my way, Heath.'

'Am I?'

He didn't move so she tried a firmer approach. 'If you want feeding you'd better get out of my way now.'

'I love it when you talk tough.'

She drew in a great, shuddering gust of relief when Heath finally straightened up and moved away. Fantasies were safe, warm things, but the reality of Heath's hard, virile body so close to hers was something else again. He hadn't even touched her yet and every part of her was glowing with lust—and she couldn't blame the Aga for that.

'Don't burn my supper,' Heath warned. 'If you do I shall have to punish you.'

Bronte drew in a sharp, shocked breath. The images that conjured up didn't even bear thinking about. Rallying, she turned to face Heath with her chin tilted at a combative angle, only to find a slow-burning smile playing around his lips. He was enjoying this. Heath was the master of verbal seduction and she was his willing partner in crime. Lucky for her, the girls chose that moment to return from the herb garden—if she counted luck in heated aches and screaming frustration, that was, Bronte mused, adopting an innocent expression by the cooker.

'Thyme?' Colleen held out a thick bunch of fragrant herbs.

'Bad time,' Heath commented dryly. Then pointing a finger at Bronte as if to say they had unfinished business, he left the kitchen to call the men.

She couldn't think of anything else all through supper. What had Heath meant by that pointing finger? If Heath meant what she thought he meant her fantasies were out of a job. Heath gave nothing away during the meal— he barely looked at her. She had cooked her heart out, silently thanking her mother for all those hours they'd spent together preparing food. She had everything she needed in the restored garden—and more eggs than she knew what to do with, thanks to the chickens being of too little value for Uncle Harry's executors to chase them down. Tonight's menu included minestrone soup, and a huge Spanish omelette, full of finely chopped seasonal vegetables and crispy potatoes, which she had browned beneath the grill until the cheese on top was crunchy. To complement this there was a bowl of crispy salad, along with some freshly baked bread and newly churned butter from a nearby farm. Then there was beer, wine and soft drinks from the local shop to satisfy twelve hungry mouths around the supper table. She loved doing this, Bronte reflected with her chin on the heel of her hand as the chatter continued abated—especially feeding Heath, who seemed to relish every mouthful.

'The country's not so bad, is it, Heath?' She couldn't resist saying when he dived in for second helpings.

'I'll freely admit it gives me a healthy appetite.'

And how was she supposed to take that? She drew a deep, steadying breath, but the tension between them remained electric. It was the same between Heath's men and Bronte's friends, she noticed. The village was severely depleted when it came to good-looking guys, as most had gone to work in the city, so this was an interesting occasion for everyone, to say the least.

'This is a real feast,' Colleen observed, passing the bread round.

Indeed it was, Bronte thought, glancing at Heath.

'Here's that cheese we bought to go with the bread,' he said, passing the cheese board round to an appreciative roar.

Bronte's glance yo-yoed between Colleen and Heath. They had walked to the farm together, which meant they must have talked. And Colleen was hardly noted for holding back. She must have said something about Bronte's feelings for Heath.

Well, it was too late to do anything about that now, Bronte thought, putting an Eton mess on the table for pudding—easy. fresh whipped and sweetened cream, thick Greek yoghurt, strawberries, raspberries, and crumbled chunks of home-made meringue. 'Please, tuck in,' she announced brightly, swallowing back her embarrassment at the thought that her feelings for Heath must have been aired extensively at some point today.

'This pudding is delicious,' Heath said, looking up.

His eyes held all sorts of thoughts that went beyond pudding—none of which Bronte trusted herself to examine too closely. How would Heath's energy translate if they were left alone together for any length of time? Perhaps he had better install a sprinkler system along with all his other DIY improvements.

'We're going to be here for the best part of six months according to the boss,' one of the men said, directing this comment at Bronte. 'I hope you'll be staying on?'

'She'll be here,' Heath confirmed.

'Oh, will I?' Bronte challenged.

'Where else would you go?' Heath demanded.

Everyone went silent and turned to look at them.

'We definitely can't let a cook as good as you go,' the first man said politely to break the standoff.

'We won't let her go,' Heath assured him while Bronte frowned. It wasn't just that she didn't like to be told what she was going to do—she was beginning to wonder if she had blown the bigger job. Not that she didn't enjoy cooking, but her mother was the one trained in household management, while Bronte's training had been geared towards managing the estate.

Don't make a fuss, her inner voice warned...*softly, softly catchee monkey.*

'I've really enjoyed cooking for you all,' she said honestly, thinking it best to leave it there.

'If you do stay on and work here,' Colleen piped up, 'I'm sure Heath will pay excellent wages.'

'We definitely need to talk terms,' Heath agreed above the laughter.

Great wages and impossible terms? Bronte smiled and kept on smiling as if she hadn't a care in the world. But when everyone started getting up from the table and she noticed Heath was looking at her, her senses sharpened. After what Heath had described as her less than promising start, she hoped she had gone some way to making amends tonight. But she still needed clarification about a formal interview—that was if Heath's offer still stood.

Her first thought was, what would the position be?

Missionary? Or up against a wall—

Stop! *Stop!*

Estate manager, or housekeeper, Bronte told herself firmly, wiping her overheated forehead on the back of her hand. She'd settle for either—though of course she would hand over the housekeeper's position to her mother, with Heath's agreement, the moment her parents returned from their trip.

She was so busy clearing the table and trying to see into the future that she managed to crash into Heath. 'Well?' he demanded, steadying her, his firm hands so warm and strong on her arms. 'I'm still waiting for your answer, Bronte.'

'Wages?'

'Terms,' he murmured.

'And is that look supposed to encourage me to accept?' His gaze was currently focused on her lips.

'I haven't offered you anything yet,' he pointed out. 'Is this a better look?'

His face was so close she could see the flecks of amber in his eyes. 'Barely,' she said.

Her body disagreed. Her body liked Heath's brooding look very much indeed. 'You can let me go now,' she said, staring pointedly at his hand on her arm.

Heath hummed as he lifted it away, leaving behind him an imprint of sensation that it would take more than a shower to wash off.

This was everything she'd ever dreamed of, Bronte reflected as she cleared the table—Heath back at Hebers Ghyll, picking up almost, but not quite, where they'd left off, flirting with him.

Flirting with Heath was a very bad idea indeed. It put her heart at risk, while his was in no danger at all. And she didn't kid herself where this was heading, if she let it. Heath had a healthy appetite, and it was up to her to decide yes or no and then take the consequences for her decision whatever it might be.

Everyone else had left the kitchen to return to work. No one stopped until a job was done now, Bronte had noticed, even thought it was quite late. Heath's influence, she supposed. He never seemed to tire. She had asked him to mend a fuse for her before he went back to join the others. 'Seems I can't get rid of you now,' she teased him as he straightened up.

'Isn't that what you want?' he said.

She was staring at his lips again, Bronte realised, shifting her gaze to Heath's work-stained top. 'Do you really think I find the scent of spark plugs and engine oil irresistible?'

'I think you love a bit of rough.'

'I—'

Before she had chance to deny it, Heath had dragged her into his arms.

'It might have escaped your notice,' she told him, coolly, 'but I'm in no danger of falling over at the moment.'

'You're right,' Heath agreed, lips pressing down. 'You're in no danger at all.' He lifted his hands away.

The master tactician was at it again, Bronte suspected, feeling the loss of him before Heath had even left the room. There was more to foreplay than she had ever realised. Turned out Heath was master of that too. Still, he'd gone now, which would give her chance to cool down. She'd clear up the kitchen—and then, as she'd announced over supper, she would paint the wall Heath had plastered. The plaster had dried out now, and she didn't feel like going down to the pub. Sometimes she liked to be alone with her thoughts—though where that would get her tonight was anyone's guess.

CHAPTER SEVEN

EVERYONE was going down to the pub in the village after work. Heath wasn't and neither was Bronte. She was still fixing up the kitchen. Having cooked and cleaned and cleared, she had declared her intention to paint the wall. He could hardly leave her to it.

Stubborn as ever, he thought, catching sight of her through the kitchen window. It looked cosy and welcoming inside with the lights casting a warm glow, and something Bronte had prepared for tomorrow bubbling away quietly on the Aga. She was up a ladder with her hair tied back beneath a bright emerald-green scarf— and she was wielding a roller—

God help them all. Cream paint extended down to her elbow, and there was a smudge of it on her nose. He'd better get in there before she painted herself to the wall.

'Knock it off now, Bronte,' he said as he walked into the room. 'It's almost nine o' clock.'

'Past your bedtime?' she teased him.

He wasn't even remotely tired.

Turning, she planted her hands on her hips, daubing her jeans with another generous lashing of paint.

'I hope that paint washes off.'

'You know something, Heath,' she said thoughtfully.

'You said I'd made a bad start. Well, now I'm wondering if I want a job here at all. The thought of you bossing me around all day and all night—'

'Is irresistible,' he said, easing onto one hip to stare up at her. 'You know you'd love it. Just think—you'd be able to argue with me non-stop.'

She sighed. 'Sadly, I don't have your stamina.'

Something he'd like to put to the test. But shouldn't. *Mustn't*. 'Now I know you're joking. I've seen that tongue of yours do the marathon. And, didn't I just tell you to stop?'

Her jaw dropped in mock shock. 'I obey you now?'

'Didn't I tell you that's part of the job description?' Cupping his chin, he pretended to think about it—and cursed himself for forgetting to shave. Barbarian? She was right.

She hummed. 'We may have a serious problem, in that case. Unless…'

'Unless?' he prompted.

'Unless you're offering to make me a drink?' she said perkily.

'Gin and tonic?'

'Coffee,' she said in a reproving tone.

Coffee won. Climbing down the ladder, she tried to muscle him out of the way when he took over the cooker. No contest. He was skipper of the Aga tonight. 'You can't stand the fact that I'm in charge,' he said as she bumped against him one last time and finally gave up. 'You've grown wild on your travels—uncontrollable—you've got no discipline—you're answerable to no one—'

'But you love me,' she said, adding quickly in her sensible voice to cover for her gaffe. 'I'm answerable to myself, Heath. And I learned a lot while I was away.'

He didn't doubt it, and while she took the pan off the cooker and washed out the paintbrushes he encouraged her to tell him something about her extended trip. So much of it turned out to be relevant to the job of estate manager at Hebers Ghyll, he couldn't help but put his baser instincts on the back burner as he listened. It was fascinating to hear how she'd gone from naïve, untried miss, to Capability Bronte, building fences, birthing animals, and helping to construct artesian wells along the way. He revised his opinion of her upwards another good few notches when she told him, 'Life's easy when there's no responsibility attached. I needed to get out there, Heath. I had to get away from this small village— not just to find out what I was missing, but to test myself and find out what I'm made of.'

'Sugar and spice and all things nice?'

'Now, you know that's not true,' she told him, smiling.

'So did you find the missing link?'

She thought about it for a moment. 'I discovered how much I love it here,' she said, biting the full swell of her bottom lip, as if lust for travel and the love of home were warring inside her.

'You love a lot,' he observed.

'How do you work that out?'

'You talk about love all the time, but love isn't a cure-all, Bronte.'

'Maybe not,' she said, 'but nothing much would get done without it.'

He held up his hands to that. 'Did you love teaching me to read?'

She held his gaze for a moment in silence as if she knew that everything that mattered to him would be contained in her answer. 'I loved being with you,' she said steadily. 'And you were a good student,' she added thoughtfully.

'And now?'

'I don't think I could teach you anything,' she said honestly.

'Well, thank you, ma'am.' He curved a grin. 'I can't believe you said that—'

'I can't believe it, either,' she agreed, and then they both laughed. And moved one step closer.

'I haven't had your education,' he admitted as she started clearing up.

'You've had plenty at the school of life,' she observed. And when she turned to him her face was serious. 'You had more schooling in that university than most people could deal with, Heath.'

They said nothing for a moment and then he curved a grin and let it go.

'This paint is supposed to wash off easily,' she grumbled from the sink, up to her elbows in soapy water.

'Am I allowed to smile?' he said.

'You do what you want from what I've seen.'

She turned back to vigorously washing her hands again, but not before he'd seen the blood rush to her cheeks. 'Towel?' he suggested.

'Please.'

He made coffee and passed her a mug. She hummed appreciatively and started sipping.

'Good?'

Emerald eyes found him over the rim of the mug. 'Very good—you're a man of many talents, Heath.'

'I'm a businessman. I do what I have to—as efficiently as I can.'

'But you are growing to love it here, aren't you?' she

asked him, unable to keep the anxiety out of her voice. 'Just a little bit, anyway?'

'Nothing would entice me to subscribe to your woolly view that love changes everything, Bronte. Do you seriously think love would be enough here?'

'Obviously, Hebers Ghyll needs a little more help than loving thoughts,' she conceded.

'Help from a jaded city type like me, possibly?'

'A man with enough money to make things happen? Yes, that should do it,' she agreed, brazen as you like.

A long-time fan of Bronte's directness, he wasn't fazed, and went in with a challenge of his own. 'And the sparring between us? Could we work round that?'

'I'd find a way to deal with it,' she said, frowning.

Was she thinking about the fun they could have making up?

'The only reason I'm here,' she assured him seriously, 'is to make sure you don't knock the place down when no one's looking.'

'And build a shopping centre?' He laughed. 'And, of course, that's the only reason you're here?'

'There's no other reason I can think of.'

Opening the fridge, he took out a beer, knocked the top off the bottle on the edge of the kitchen table, and chugged it down. 'I'm not a man who destroys things, Bronte—when will you get that through your head? I'm a builder by nature, and a games designer by trade. I see no conflict there. I create things. Cyber worlds, brick walls—they're all the same to me; it's what I do.'

'But your life is in the city, Heath. So you wouldn't stay here year round—and whoever makes a success of Hebers Ghyll would have to love it enough to live here.'

'Every second of every day?' He shrugged. 'I don't think so. That's what a good estate manager's for.'

Bronte fell silent as this sank in. Even if she won the job there would be no Heath.

'You can't run a place like Hebers Ghyll on good intentions, Bronte. Look at Uncle Harry—'

'Yes. Look at him,' she said fiercely.

And now they were both quiet.

She was moving their mugs to the sink one minute—the next she had grabbed the paintbrush, jabbed it in the paint-tray and come looking for him.

'You want a fight, do you?' he challenged, dodging out of her way.

So much, Bronte thought.

'You deserved that,' she told him, backing off having given Heath a stripe of paint across his arm.

'Did I?' He circled round her. 'The countryside is just a lot of empty space to me,' he taunted. 'Just think of all those potential building plots—'

'Stop it,' she warned him, making another lunge, which he just managed to evade.

'The noise and the rush of the city?' He backed her slowly towards the wall as he pretended to think about it. 'Or the silence and emptiness of the countryside? Hmm. Let me think...'

'Empty?' she exclaimed, making a double stab at him before slipping away under his arm. 'The countryside empty? You should open your eyes and look around, Heath.'

He wiped the paint off his cheek. 'My eyes are wide open, believe me,' he assured her, moving in for the kill.

'I don't know why you even came here,' she said as

he held her firmly with the brush dangling a tempting inch or two from her face.

'Profit, wasn't it?' he growled, easing her wrist so the brush laid a dainty paint trail across her cheek.

'Why, you—'

'Barbarian?' he suggested, directing the brush across her nose.

'I'll never forgive you for this.'

He wasn't concerned. Bronte's eyes told him something very different—and so did the swell of her mouth. He wouldn't leave a paint trail there, he decided, removing the paintbrush from her hand and putting it in the sink. That would definitely be against his best interests. 'I'm confiscating this,' he said, running water over the brush. Next, he dampened a cloth. 'And now I'm going to clean you up.' He raised a challenging brow when she threatened to resist him.

'I should go,' she said breathlessly, one step ahead of him as she stared at the door.

'No,' he argued softly, 'you should come.'

She drew in a sharp breath as she turned to look at him. 'Is everything a joke to you, Heath?'

'Is this a joke?' Wielding the warm, moist cloth with the utmost care, he swung an arm around her shoulder to draw her close and wiped the paint smears off her face. 'I've made a decision,' he murmured, noting the rapid rise and fall of her chest as her breathing speeded up.

'Have you?' There was only the smallest ring of vivid green around her pupils as she stared at him. 'This will all be worth it if I have persuaded you to keep Hebers Ghyll, Heath.'

He smiled into her eyes. 'Sorry to disappoint. The most I'm prepared to commit to at this moment in time is that I will keep the place alive and continue with the renovations. Don't look so surprised,' he teased. 'A demolition site is worth far less to me than a stately home.'

'I'll get the paint again,' she threatened him.

'Then I'd just have to wash you all over again...'

Her eyes widened. 'You wouldn't dare.'

'Are you sure of that?'

'What do I have to do to stop you?'

He didn't miss the note of pent-up excitement in her voice.

'Everything I tell you,' he murmured.

'What's the catch?' she said suspiciously.

'There is no catch.'

'Then tell me what I have to do—' She followed his gaze to the door. 'Heath, we can't—'

'Why not?' Angling his chin, he stared down at her.

'Because it's outrageous,' she whispered, her voice trembling with excitement.

'You don't do outrageous?' Dipping his head, he kissed her neck.

CHAPTER EIGHT

HEATH's hand cupped Bronte's chin. He made her look at him. She could see in his gaze what came next and how incredible it was going to be. His hand felt warm and gentle on her face. For such a big man, Heath could be incredibly sensitive—and intuitive. It was this mix of soothing balm and fiery passion she craved now. She was hungry for tenderness. Only-child syndrome, maybe, Bronte thought. With both her parents working there hadn't been much time to spare for cuddling. And though there had been other children visiting Hebers Ghyll she'd always felt on the outside looking in—except with Heath. They had both been different, she supposed—the dreamer and the wild boy from the city.

'Hey, come back to me,' Heath insisted.

She looked at him. They could both have used a hug back then. She had always been hungry for Heath. He had lit a fire no amount of common sense could hope to put out, and that fire had been smouldering for thirteen years. Could anything stand in its way now?

'This isn't so outrageous, is it?' Heath demanded, tightening his grip on her when she exhaled shakily.

'You're a very bad man indeed.'

Heath smiled, and then his lips brushed her cheek.

He was making her tremble. He was making the ache inside her turn into a primitive hunger that lacked every vestige of romance.

And then he brought her in front of him and Heath's steady gaze didn't leave her eyes as his hands moved slowly down her arms. He could read every thought and she felt violently exposed, yet glad that Heath could see her hunger for him. She exclaimed softly when his thumb pad caught the tip of her nipple—but it moved on. This was all intended. Heath had caught her in his erotic net. And she wasn't interested in escaping. She was only interested in what came next.

Heath's hand was moving lightly down her spine towards her buttocks. Her breathing sounded ragged as that experienced hand continued on, and when it reached the hollow in the small of her back it fitted so neatly, she relaxed, but when he moved on to map the swell of her bottom that was too much. With a shaking cry, she arched her back, offering herself for pleasure. Heath's hands maintained a detailed exploration—sensitively seeking, and yet never quite giving her the contact she craved. 'Oh, please—' She was shivering with anticipation, shameless in her need. 'Please don't tease me like this, Heath.'

Heath said nothing as he continued to stroke and prepare. Her breathing sounded noisy in the silence, and she knew he must feel her heat through the flimsy protection of her clothes. She was moist and swollen— ready for him, and the only thought in her head was, Don't stop.

'And if I stop now?' Heath said, pausing.

'Have you read my mind?' She heard the smile in his voice, and could picture the curve of Heath's lips, even with her face buried in the soft wool of his sweater. 'You can't stop now,' she said, gazing up at him, 'Because I can't stop now.'

'So, what's the answer?' he said, frowning.

'You have to kiss me.'

'Is that a command?' Heath's lips curved with amusement.

'Yes, please,' she said.

Maybe her memory of all those years back was faulty. Maybe one kiss would be the answer to resisting Heath—to resisting what her body begged her to do.

His mouth was so close her lips tingled. She sighed, climbing to the next level of arousal as Heath brushed his lips against hers. Reaching up, she laced her fingers through his hair, opening her body to a man more than capable of taking advantage of her. Her legs were trembling against his. She'd waited so long. Heath didn't disappoint. His kiss was firm and sure, and the touch of his hands on her body was indescribable. Heat ran through her like a torrent of molten lava, and when he teased her lips apart with his tongue she was glad of his arms supporting her. Hunger ruled her. She was captive to feelings so strong it was impossible to keep them in check. Breath shot from her lungs as Heath's grip tightened. She wanted him. She wanted to share his warmth and confidence. She wanted his body. She wanted Heath to take hold of her and position her as he pleasured her, and for him to go on pleasuring her until the world and all its uncertainties faded away.

There could be no more delays. She had no inhibitions left—no restraint. There was just an urgent need to feel Heath hot and hard inside her. She wanted him as a wild animal wanted its mate. There was nothing tender about this—no thought, no reason, just a glorious battle with one sure ending. Naked flesh on naked flesh, drugging and intoxicating—no kisses, no tender promises, only now.

She rejoiced in the rasp of Heath's chest hair against her pitifully sensitive nipples, and welcomed him, hard, hot and savage against her. She cried out with excitement when he brought her jeans down in one swift move and lifted her. 'Now,' she instructed him, crazy with need.

'Not so fast,' Heath murmured. His experienced hands had found her, checked that she was ready, and then he quickly protected them both.

She locked her legs around his waist. 'Oh, no...no... no,' she cried, shaking her head wildly from side to side as he started teasing her with just the tip.

'Oh, yes...yes,' Heath responded, taking her deep.

Her eyes widened. She gasped with astonishment at the size of him. She gripped his shoulder for support. Planting her hands flat against his chest, she braced herself—and when the pleasure became too great, she laced her fingers through his hair, threw her head back and rode the sensation. This was so much more than she had expected. She was lost in pleasure, lost to reason. Heath was every bit as intuitive as she'd known he would be, and infinitely sensitive to her needs. He must never stop, she thought wildly as he dealt her the deep rhythmical strokes. She wouldn't let him stop. She was floating on an erotic plane where she had nothing to do but accept pleasure while Heath, with one hand braced against the door, pounded into her.

'You're fantastic,' she screamed at the moment of release. As she collapsed against him she realised this was true. Heath was an extraordinary lover, and she was addicted to his very special brand of pleasure. She pressed her face against his chest, inhaling his warm, clean male scent. Heath was everything she had ever wanted in a man—everything she had ever dreamed he would be. He was so tender and careful as he lowered her to the floor. He didn't let go of her until he was sure she was steady on her feet; by that time her heart was full of him.

'Better?' he murmured, smiling against her hair.

'Transformed,' she told him. That was nothing more than the truth. She could hardly believe what had happened, and was so glad that it had.

'Until the next time?' Heath's voice was full of the affection she longed to hear as he nuzzled his face against her neck.

'We belong together, you and I, I've always known it,' she said, snuggling into him. Perhaps Heath did too. He'd said until the next time, which couldn't be long now, she thought, gazing up at him. She only needed a couple of minutes to recover, and then she'd be—

Something had changed, Bronte realised, feeling sick inside. She'd said too much as usual, and Heath had changed. She had frightened him off with her big emotions. She could feel the change in his body—in his stillness—in his drawing back. His hard frame was unyielding when seconds ago it had been hers. A chill ran through her at the thought that while she had been spinning like a dervish out of control, Heath had been quietly thinking.

But what they'd done wasn't wrong.

However many times she told herself this, it didn't change the way Heath had become. Hard flesh that had moulded her soft body was just hard flesh, and the sensitive hands that had catered to her every need while Heath held her safe had grown light and impersonal. 'Heath?'

He didn't move for a moment, as if he respected the

fact that they both needed a moment to come down and grow accustomed to this change between them. He might as well have left the room, Bronte thought.

'Okay?' he said at last, dropping a kiss on the top of her head.

'I'm fine,' she said as if she were reassuring him.

While she got herself sorted out she could hear Heath fastening his jeans and securing his belt. How quiet they were—how reserved…like two strangers. She didn't need anyone to tell her they'd got it wrong. The knowledge hung between them in the air. And into a mind that didn't want to accept the truth, she knew that sex—for that was all it had been with Heath—had been a terrible mistake, and that she must cut her feelings for him now before they swamped her. A relationship with a man like Heath was never going anywhere, so it was better to end it and show how sophisticated she could be before she ruined her chances of ever being taken seriously as a candidate for the job. She huffed lightly. 'To think I only asked for coffee.'

'I promised the lads I'd join them later,' Heath said, picking up on her change of mood. 'Are you sure you'll be okay if I go?'

As he spoke he reached out a hand, and she sensed Heath wanted to stroke her hair. She pulled back. There was nothing temperamental or dramatic about it, this was just a signal between friends that they understood each other. 'Of course I'll be okay,' she said. 'Why shouldn't I be? I'm just going to finish up in here, and then I'm going home for a long, hot bath and a lazy night in front of the TV.'

'If you're sure?' Heath looked puzzled.

'Are you sure you're all right?' she countered wryly. 'I can walk you to the pub, if you like?'

'I think I'll be safe,' Heath answered in the same ironic tone.

'Okay.' Angling her chin, she found a smile.

She waited until he left the room and then blew out a long, slow breath. Behave with dignity, she told herself firmly. She had wanted Heath—and had been determined to have him. And now she had, she must take the consequences.

So that was settled.

Good.

Hearing the outer door closing, she listened to Heath's footsteps crossing the yard. Even they were unbearably familiar, but gradually they faded. Bronte only hoped her feelings would do the same. Closing her eyes, she gave it a moment. No change. Still acting calmly, she was screaming in her head. There was no right way to handle this. Well, there was, as far as the outside world was concerned and Heath, but for her tonight was a memory to lock away, and to get out and examine whenever she needed to beat herself up.

But she couldn't stand here for ever feeling sorry for herself, Bronte concluded. Her feet might appear to be superglued to the floor, but even she couldn't live off emotion. It wouldn't decorate the kitchen any more than it would save Hebers Ghyll—both would need more direct action. And at least with decorating there was more certainty of success, she thought, picking up her brush. Men could punch the wall when things went wrong, but she'd settle for prising open a new can of cream paint. If she finished the wall tonight then at least something would have reached a satisfactory conclusion.

He didn't go to the pub or anywhere near it. He got straight in the car and drove back to the city. When he reached the open road he stamped his foot down on the accelerator. The hunger to put miles between him and Bronte was as fierce as the hunger that had flared between them. She was like a wild green shoot that couldn't survive his brand of tough. Beneath Bronte's fire there was tenderness and vulnerability. He'd always known it and couldn't forgive himself for what had happened. Bronte embraced life and all it had to offer, but her enthusiasm was coloured by the desperate hope that no one would hurt her—but they would. He would. And so he was leaving.

Heath grimaced as he roughly brushed a stubble-roughened chin against his arm. What the hell had he been thinking? Bronte was as innocent as she had ever been. And he had never been innocent. If he owed Uncle Harry anything, it was not to pursue this madness—this hunger—this…Bronte.

But even when he tried to clear his mind she was still in there—her fresh wildflower scent lingering, mingled with paint fumes. He could still see the humour in her eyes, and the determined jut of her chin…that stubborn mouth. That stubborn, kissable mouth—

He actually groaned out loud at this point. He should never have come to the country. He belonged in town. The only thing he could be thankful for right now was that his utility vehicle was eating up the narrow lanes with an appetite he shared. The sooner he replaced green fields and Bronte with a reassuring cityscape of concrete and uncomplicated women, the sooner he'd relax—

Was that right?

When Bronte had shaken him in so many ways? She'd touched on feelings he'd managed to successfully beat down for years. She'd left him questioning more than just his relationship with Uncle Harry and Hebers Ghyll.

She had reminded him of things he'd been ashamed of, and turned them into something to celebrate. She was the first woman to match his sexual appetite. The first woman to whom he had felt seriously attracted. The first woman he had ever come close to considering a friend—

Bronte's vulnerability stopped him dead in his tracks every time. Seeing that was the only warning he needed that this madness had to stop. They weren't meeting on an even playing field, or anything like. Bronte cared too much about everything—and she hadn't fooled him with her casual act. Bronte wore her heart on her sleeve—which was lovely, but not when he was involved. It would be too easy for him to trample her heart. And not intentionally. That was just the way he was. He had never made room in his life for emotion. He was stone to Bronte's soul. He had nothing to offer her. But he wouldn't break his promise. He had assumed responsibility for Hebers Ghyll, and that wouldn't change. And he would give her a shot at the job.

Dealing with Bronte on a professional basis would be different, Heath convinced himself as industrial units encroached on the fields, reminding him that his journey was coming to an end. He would be in control if and when she worked for him. Emotion had no part to play. Poverty had made him a stickler for control dating back to when he'd made his first big money and realised the changes he could make. He had controlled the spending to make sure not a penny of his hard-earned cash was wasted. He couldn't delegate. He had never learned to relax.

More reasons why he could never be the man Bronte wanted him to be. She wasn't even his type, Heath reasoned, stamping down on the accelerator as the lights changed. Her dress sense alone was bad enough—

To keep the thought of yanking Bronte's clothes off her at the forefront of his mind at all times.

He curved a smile—and then reminded himself about his good intentions. They were soon dispatched. But then there was The Temper. Wasn't that just what he needed? Why couldn't he meet some nice, compliant girl?

Because they bored him, Heath reasoned, swinging the wheel as he turned onto the six-lane highway leading into the city. That certainty only grew when he remembered the squads of eager candidates with their porcelain smiles and improbably inflated breasts. It made him smile to think those flutterbys had been effortlessly eclipsed by a tiny, passionate girl—so real, so true, he doubted he could ever go back to plastic.

She usually woke up and leapt out of bed at the cottage full of bounce because there was so much to do at Hebers Ghyll, and she so wanted to get there and do it—but not this morning. This morning she felt flat.

Because there was a whole world of beating herself up to do, Bronte realised as she crawled out of bed. She was still aching from Heath's spectacular attentions, and only wished she could feel differently about what had happened. But she couldn't. It still felt so right to her, though clearly Heath hadn't felt the same.

Heath was right. Get on with your life, Bronte reasoned as she walked down the now neatly manicured drive towards the hall. It was such a beautiful morning she wouldn't let anything get her down—

Where was Heath's truck?

Bronte's heart plummeted as she quickly raced

through all the possibilities, ending in the feeble: perhaps Heath had left early to get some supplies…

That wasn't the answer. She was just putting off the moment when she had to face the truth. Lifting her chin, she took a moment to steel herself before facing the others. She was her old self again by the time she let herself into the house—as far as anyone else could tell.

The kitchen was empty.

So empty.

With just a faint smell of non-smell paint. The first thing she did was open the window to let some fresh air in.

What had she expected, Bronte asked herself, gripping the edge of the table—Heath waiting with a bunch of flowers and a cheesy grin? Did that sound like Heath? He had never planned to stay long. And he had never misled her. If anything, she was surprised he had stayed in the countryside as long as he had. Heath ran a highly successful business in the city. Hebers Ghyll was just a hobby for him. He'd come down when he could spare the time, he'd said.

If all those elegant women queuing up to go to bed with him could spare him—

She mustn't think like that, Bronte scolded herself fiercely. What had happened last night was nothing more than the result of working in close proximity with a very attractive man. It was normal—natural. She was a free agent—she could do what she liked. And she liked what had happened last night. A lot. And what Heath chose to do in his own time was Heath's business. And—

And, damn it, she was crying.

CHAPTER NINE

DASHING her tears away impatiently, Bronte got the morning underway—putting the kettle on, slicing bread for toast. She had breakfast to cook, thank goodness. There was so much she had to do that would take her mind off Heath.

The laugh she gave now was poor competition for the whistling kettle. It was a horrid, weak, sniffly sort of laugh. She couldn't forget him. She couldn't let it lie here. As soon as everyone had finished breakfast she was going to ring Heath's PA and ask about the interviews. The job of estate manager at Hebers Ghyll was going begging, and no one else was going to muscle in while she was mooching around here feeling sorry for herself.

Bronte was stunned when Heath's PA rang her first. She was still tidying the kitchen, and had to sit down on a chair to take the call. Shocked? She was incredulous he'd even remembered her. Interviews for the post of estate manager had been arranged for the following week in their London offices, the posh guy called Quentin told her, and he was calling to make sure she was still interested.

'Absolutely,' she confirmed, branding the date and time of the interview on her mind.

Getting up, she paced the room. What did this mean? Did Heath miss her? Did he want her back?

Desperate twit, she thought, drawing to a halt to stare out of the window at the yard where Heath had put on his spectacular wet torso display. This wasn't about Bronte and Heath. This was about the job of estate manager. Heath had promised her this chance to attend a formal interview—why would he take that away? What would be the point? She was well qualified—a good contender; she had to hope the best. The fact that Heath had asked his PA to call her rather than doing it himself only proved that he wanted to keep things on a strictly business footing. It was the right thing to do. It was what she would have done had their roles been reversed, she told herself firmly. This was her chance to prove she was as professional as Heath—and a chance to tilt at a job she desperately wanted. If she was lucky enough to land the job it would be the best chance she ever got to take Uncle Harry's vision to the next level—and to prove she was more than Heath's latest sex-starved admirer.

She could do this.

She must do this, Bronte determined, firming her jaw.

'Did you call her?' Heath's tone was impatient. Almost as soon as he'd returned to London he'd had to fly to New York—one of his favourite cities, but waiting to get out of this meeting with his lawyers hadn't helped to soothe his frayed temper.

'Of course,' Quentin confirmed. 'I made it my first job—I even placed the call before I drank my coffee.'

'I appreciate the sacrifice,' Heath said dryly, but then the crease returned to his brow. 'What did she say?'

'She's coming.'

Heath relaxed back on the sofa overlooking Central Park. He hadn't shaved. He hadn't even showered yet. It felt like he hadn't slept for days. His emergency meeting had been called to sew up a deal that would take his company global. He'd texted Quentin to make the date with Bronte, thumbs racing beneath the table as he discussed figures the size of a roll-over lottery win at the same time. He had promised Bronte this chance, and he was a man of his word.

And that was the only reason he'd called her to interview, he'd told himself sternly when he stood to shake hands with the other men. It had absolutely nothing to do with the fact that all he'd thought of since leaving England, in those moments when the business relaxed its hold on him, was Bronte—Bronte's eyes, the swell of her mouth, the expression on her face, the sound of her voice when she was out of control with pleasure in his arms, or whispering to him in the aftermath. Most of all he wondered about the questions she never asked him, like, Why does it have to be like this, Heath? Why must the past always stand between us? Why can't you and I be together like any other couple? We enjoyed the sex—we're so good together, why can't it go on? And then the lies she would tell him if he let things run on. He could hear her saying, sex doesn't have to involve feelings, does it, Heath? Then she would look at him with those candid green eyes and they would both know she was lying. He couldn't hurt her like that. Sex had to involve feelings for Bronte. Everything had to involve feelings for Bronte.

When the lawyers from both sides shook hands and turned to congratulate him, he barely heard them. All he could think of was a long, reviving shower and the welcome journey home. For Bronte's sake, he'd shave.

Right now he looked more the barbarian than ever and he didn't want to frighten her when she interviewed for the job—he owed her that much. The interview was all she had ever asked of him, and he wouldn't let her down.

It was just her bad luck that Heath's office was located in the most fashionable part of the city, Bronte reflected, slipping on a robe after her shower at the cottage. And in a gleaming new building that had won style awards, for goodness' sake.

And look at me...

So she would just have to smarten herself up, Bronte told herself firmly. It might have been a while, but she could do it. Taking a deep breath, she stopped pacing her bedroom to open the robe and take a critical look at herself in the full-length mirror. The bits that showed outside her dungarees were tanned to a nice healthy shade, but the rest of her was pale and freckled.

And the tip of her nose was bright red.

Great.

Walking to the wardrobe, she opened the door and rooted inside. It wasn't that she didn't know how to dress or what would be expected of her at a high-powered interview. She hadn't dropped out of life completely, but she had gone country. There had been no reason to smarten up since she'd returned to Hebers Ghyll.

There wasn't time to buy a business suit, Bronte concluded, but appearances were everything if she wanted Heath to take her seriously. Appearances were important if she wanted to hold her head up high. Toe rings and braids she had down to a fine art, but a more sophisticated look might require a little help...

* * *

'You're going to Heath's office for an interview?' Colleen exclaimed, clearly impressed and excited for her. 'That's amazing. Heath must think a lot of you to invite you down to London.'

'That's where the interviews are being held,' Bronte explained. 'It's nothing special. And it was his PA who invited me, not Heath.'

'Whatever you say...'

They were clearing out the old stables when Bronte shared her news. Colleen had picked up on her tension, Bronte realised.

Leaning on her sweeping brush, Colleen stared directly at her equally dishevelled friend. 'So, tell me—what can I do?'

'I'm just worried that the job of estate manager suggests someone older than me—someone more staid.'

'I disagree,' Colleen said firmly. 'You're the new generation.'

'But what if Heath's PA doesn't see it that way? What if I don't get any further than him? He sounds so snooty, and appearances matter in the city. I don't think my muck-spreading look is going to cut it.'

'You might have a point,' Colleen agreed with a laugh as she took in the state of Bronte's dungarees. 'So you really think you've got a chance of landing the job? It would be wonderful if you did—it would give everyone such a lift.'

'Thanks,' Bronte said, smiling ruefully. 'I have to believe I stand a chance or I wouldn't go to London. I've got the right qualifications—and the right practical experience too. And I've got local knowledge, which hopefully will give me an edge. So, logically, I should be in the running...' Though whether Mr Logical would see it that way remained to be seen. 'But I must look as professional as I can, which is where you come in.'

'Whatever I can do,' Colleen offered.

'Well, I've been off the radar for a while—so I'll need a suit.'

'And there are so many shops round here,' Colleen said dryly.

'Exactly, and there's no time to visit the local town before my interview.'

'Well, you must look good for Heath.'

'This has nothing to do with Heath,' Bronte protested a little too hotly.

'Okay,' Colleen soothed, holding her hands up palms flat in surrender.

'Heath needs to come back to oversee this project,' Bronte said thoughtfully. 'An absentee landlord is no good to Hebers Ghyll.'

'And an absentee lover is even less use to you.'

'Colleen—'

'I'm just saying. If friends can't be honest with each other. Yes, of course I'll help,' Colleen confirmed when Bronte gave her a look. 'Do you really think you can persuade Heath to come back here?'

'He has to—look how much got done on his last visit. We have to be positive, Colleen. What?' she said when Colleen's gaze slid away.

'I just don't want to see you getting hurt, Bronte.'

'I'm not going to get hurt,' Bronte said firmly. 'I know what I'm doing. This is business. Let's get back to work, shall we? I can raid your wardrobe later.'

'You can take whatever you want,' Colleen assured her.

'Then that's settled,' Bronte said cheerfully, but her friend's concerned expression hadn't changed.

* * *

The trade journals had picked up on his coup and were going crazy. The office was going crazy—and more crazy was exactly what he didn't need. 'What do you mean, you can't cope?' Heath thundered to the only man who didn't quail when he let rip.

'If I didn't work with a bloody genius, you'd know,' Heath's harassed PA informed him testily. 'You think everyone can work at your speed, Heath—i.e. the speed of light. Well, I've got news for you—I've only got one pair of hands—'

'And if you spent less time slathering hand cream on them you'd have more time to spare for work.'

'Woo-hoo. *Bitchee*. Now who's suffering from a bad dose of Not Getting Any?'

'And since when is that your business?'

'I've made it my business. I have to suffer the backlash every day.'

'If you weren't—'

'The only gay male friend you're ever likely to have?' Quentin interrupted smoothly.

'The only friend I'm likely to have,' Heath confessed ruefully.

Reaching up on tiptoe, Quentin threw a comforting arm around his boss's powerful shoulders. 'Take it from one who knows—you need to sort out that other problem first.'

'I'm working on it.'

'Good, then perhaps you'll calm down and stop carrying on like a bull with a sore head and we can get some work done around here.'

'Get some help.'

Quentin pouted. 'Now I'm offended.'

'I mean, go get someone in to handle the interviews if you can't cope.'

'Oh, I see.' Quentin smiled at the small victory as he examined his immaculately manicured nails. 'Maybe a temp to handle some of the run-of-the-mill work, while I supervise the interviews. What?' he protested. 'Did you seriously think I'd allow anyone but me to start the interview process for such a vital position on your lordship's new estate?'

'Firstly, I'm not a lord—and believe me,' Heath added dryly, 'Hebers Ghyll is not the dream property you seem to imagine, Quentin. I've seen better slums in my time.'

'And you've handled that sort of renovation perfectly. You'll handle this,' Quentin said, refusing to be dismayed.

'Maybe,' Heath growled. 'Well? What are you waiting for? Get on with it.'

Quentin gave him a mock bow. 'The master speaks and I obey.'

Heath cracked a smile. 'Now find me an estate manager who thinks the same way you do.'

Quentin pulled a hurt face. 'I can assure you, I am a one-off.'

'And I couldn't do without you,' Heath admitted.

'But I know what I'd do without you,' Quentin shot back.

'And what's that?'

'Save money at the salon—the stress lines I've developed since I started working for you—'

'And no, you can't charge your treatments to expenses.'

Quentin sulked for around a second. 'I'll get that temp in, then.'

'Yes, you do that,' Heath advised, returning to his screen.

* * *

She had never been put through such a gruelling grilling. Heath's PA, a man who went by the name of Quentin Carew, turned out to be the most formidable style maven Bronte had ever encountered, and he would be conducting the first screening process, Quentin had informed her.

Then she was out, Bronte thought. She didn't stand a chance. Quentin was infinitely better groomed than she would ever be, and Heath's offices far surpassed anything that even Bronte's lively imagination could have conjured up. A celebration of steel and glass, they were formidably smart, as was Quentin, whereas she—even with Colleen's best and kindest efforts—wasn't. But for some reason, Quentin seemed to like her. It was possible he could see right through her carefully subdued grooming and controlled manner to something quirky underneath. Perhaps it was the small heart tattoo on her wrist—something she had hoped her respectable shirt cuff would cover, but hadn't, and she had caught Quentin staring at it.

'I'm putting you through,' he announced.

'You are?' She couldn't have been more surprised, or more delighted. This was everything she had ever wanted—and was nothing at all to do with seeing Heath again, Bronte told her racing heart firmly.

'Heath could arrive at any time this afternoon,' Quentin explained, 'and as you probably know by now he can be a little…unpredictable? With a certain type of volatile…'

'Temperament?' Bronte supplied innocently.

'You might say that. I couldn't possibly comment,' Quentin remarked, picking imaginary lint off the lapels of his immaculate jacket.

The lengths some PAs will go to in order to protect

the boss, Bronte thought wryly. 'Thank you,' she said. 'And thank you for giving me this opportunity.'

'I don't know why you're thanking me,' Quentin exclaimed, confiding, 'Working here must have put at least ten years on me.'

'And you're looking great on it,' she said, smiling.

'Yes, well…' Quentin's beautifully etched lips tightened in a pout. 'That's no thanks to the man I work for.'

'Heath…' Bronte floated off into her favourite dream, and just as quickly dragged herself back again. She had to. There was a dangerous little capsule living in her mind that threatened to explode into infinite pieces of lust, self-reproach, and longing, given half a chance. And that would be too distracting when she wanted to concentrate on landing this job.

'Yes, Heath,' Quentin agreed, looking at Bronte closely. 'I should warn you that when he arrives it will be like a force ten storm hitting. You'd do well to be prepared.'

'I am prepared,' Bronte lied as her heart went crazy, knowing she could never be prepared to see Heath again.

'And you do understand that this is a high-powered office where we work at warp speed all the time?'

'I do,' Bronte confirmed, recalling the speed at which Heath could work.

'I doubt Heath will expect anything less of his staff in the country—and if he does, let me know,' Quentin added with an over-the-rim-of-his-glasses look. 'I might want to try out for a job there. I've always thought I'd look rather good in plus fours…'

'If I get the job I'll let you know,' Bronte promised as Quentin went off into his own private dreamworld.

Heath definitely hadn't let his PA into the full story at
Hebers Ghyll. An outfit of plus fours—quaint knick-
erbockers—teamed with a beautifully tailored tweed
jacket and possibly a deerstalker hat was the clothing of
choice for another type of country estate altogether—
one where the visitors would expect everything to be
sanitised and mud-free.

Shrewd blue eyes, enhanced by the most discreet
hint of grey eyeshadow, switched channels to Bronte.
'From what I've seen of your CV you should be in with
a serious chance for this job.' But now Quentin grew
concerned. 'Are you sure that working for metrosaurus-
man won't be too traumatic for you?'

'Absolutely not,' Bronte confirmed confidently. The
work wouldn't be too much for her. *But Heath*…Heath
was another story, and one that had forbidden written
all over it.

'I wouldn't normally put someone as young as you
through, but your CV is so strong,' Quentin observed.

'Thank you.' Why was Quentin looking at her like
that? Bronte wondered, growing increasingly self-
conscious. 'I normally wear jeans or dungarees,' she
explained awkwardly, conscious that her borrowed outfit
wasn't up to Quentin's standards.

'I don't doubt it,' Quentin said, confirming Bronte's
suspicions. 'But Heath is all about the city. He's tuned
into the pace of life here. Naturally, Heath can set his
own standards, but he expects—no,' Quentin said frowning, 'Heath takes for granted the fact that his employees
will dress a certain way. I'm only trying to help,' he de-
fended when Bronte gave him a hard stare. 'I just think
you'd stand a much better chance of getting this job if
you conform to the sort of look Heath will be expecting.
That's all I'm saying,' he said, raising his hands.

And she should be grateful someone as savvy as Quentin was giving her advice. She liked him. And now it was time to place her trust in him. 'I've never conformed,' she explained. 'So I'm not that sure how to do it—how to put a look together—if you know what I mean?' Quentin's interest sparked as she added, 'I don't suppose you could you help me...?'

Quentin's eyes narrowed speculatively as he looked her over. 'I could help,' he said thoughtfully, chin in hand. 'If you don't mind missing lunch...'

Bronte was round the desk in a flash. Anything to take her mind off meeting Heath.

'Heath has seen you in casual attire, I've no doubt,' Quentin pondered out loud as he walked round Bronte like a sergeant major on parade. 'It's time for him to see you dressed as a professional—sharp, contemporary, and of the moment.'

'Sounds interesting.'

'Sounds like a challenge,' Quentin argued.

'Well, if you're up for it, I am.'

'Budget?' Quentin enquired discreetly.

'Whatever it takes.' She would just have to use plastic and hope her card didn't self-combust.

'Excellent.' Quentin was already at the door. 'Well, come on—what are you waiting for, girlfriend? Let's go shopping.'

CHAPTER TEN

SOME hours later with her hair freshly shampooed at Quentin's preferred salon and left to curl in wild disarray almost to her waist, dressed in a short black skirt, black opaque tights and flat Mary Janes, with a tight little top that clung like sticking plaster to her breasts, Bronte wasn't totally convinced she looked like the archetypal interviewee for the post of estate manager at Hebers Ghyll, but more importantly Quentin was pleased with her appearance and declared her ready for her interview with Heath. 'Wouldn't I have been better buying a tweed jacket, or something?' she said, feeling increasingly anxious as the moment of truth approached. Craning her neck, she stared at her bottom, which was very tightly clad indeed.

'A tweed jacket?' Quentin demanded as if she had suggested wearing a homespun jerkin. 'Certainly not. Heath is not just the cutting edge, he is the leading edge—the spear, the arrow, the—'

'Okay, okay, I'm happy,' Bronte insisted, holding up her hands.

They returned to Heath's building where Quentin told her to wait in the anteroom to Heath's corner office.

She could do this, Bronte persuaded herself nervously, her knees jiggling up and down as she perched on the very edge of one of the smart black leather couches. Though why she was dressed as if to seduce the boss, when that was the last thing she wanted...

She was here to persuade Heath she could be a top drawer estate manager. She was not losing her nerve. She would not be fixated on how aroused she was at the thought of seeing him again. She would definitely not be scanning Heath's office for likely trysting opportunities. She would forget how she had felt after sex when Heath pulled away, and how deep the feeling was that what they'd done hadn't been wrong. She would be cool and professional. They had both moved to a new place. It was a good place. It was the right place for them to be—

And then the door swung open and the breath left her lungs in a rush. Had she really thought she was ready for this? Her heart was crashing against her ribs. Her awareness levels had soared beyond the possible. Heath stood framed in the doorway like a totem to all things sexual: a deity, a yoni god, a man with eyes of stone, wearing what, on the face of it, was a casual outfit—jeans and a top—but it was the kind of easy look that reeked of money and style.

For a moment her mind was wiped clean and her mouth refused absolutely to communicate with her brain. The last time she'd seen Heath he'd been groaning— She'd been screaming— They'd been—

Thankfully, she managed to summon up an autopilot voice—faint though it was. 'Hello, Heath.'

'Bronte,' he said briskly. All business. All coldly assessing as he took in her new look.

She wasn't sure whether to be glad of Quentin's assistance or not now. Something more low-key—something more mouse-like—might have bought her enough time to state her case clearly. Heath could convey more in one sharp stare than most men could hope to communicate in a lifetime, and that wasn't always a good thing. 'I'm your three o' clock,' she said, standing before she had too much time to analyse Heath's expression.

'I'm running late—so we'll have to make this quick.'

No, we won't, Bronte thought, frowning even as her heart beat the retreat. 'I've come all this way, Heath, and I know you're going to treat me with the same consideration you've treated all the other interviewees.'

Heath's expression didn't change. He wore a brooding look Bronte found impossible to interpret, other than to say it didn't fill her with confidence. 'I hope nothing's wrong?' she said pleasantly, determined not to be fazed. 'I guessed these interviews mean your attitude towards the country has mellowed—'

'Mellowed,' Heath cut across her, raising a brow.

'Okay, not mellowed,' Bronte conceded, but to hell with trying to phrase her words carefully. They'd known each other too long for that. She had to be candid even if their relationship had been somewhat turbulent lately. 'Finding time for Hebers Ghyll can't be easy for you, but I can take those concerns away—' The flexing of a muscle in Heath's cheek made her pause. His dangerous appeal was working its magic. Steeling herself, she pushed on. 'Give me a chance, Heath. Put everything else that's happened between us since I...since you—'

'Since we?' Heath angled his chin.

He wasn't going to make this easy for her. 'Since we had sex,' she said flatly, pressing her hands out to the side as if she were pushing the memory away. 'I'm the best person for this job. All I ask is the chance to prove that to you, Heath.'

'Go on, then, tell me why.' He leaned back against the door, drinking her in as she spoke about her experience and outlined her plans for Hebers Ghyll. She was even younger than he remembered and more innocent than he cared to think about. The fiery episode in the kitchen seemed all at odds with the girl standing in front of him now. Bronte had always led with her heart, but there was something different about her today.

He had felt energy blaze between them the moment he walked into the room, but Bronte was cool now. If anything, she was cooler than he'd ever seen her. She had moved to a new level, where ironically she was almost as unreachable as he was. She intrigued him even more. She presented more of a challenge. And she might well be the right candidate for the job. He'd made enquiries in advance of this interview—taking up her references at her old college, as well as talking to people she'd worked with. Bronte was outstanding, he'd been told. She was a terrific catch for any landowner, people in the know had assured him.

Catch was about right, he thought as he stared at her. They'd known each other for what felt like for ever— they knew each other intimately, yet they didn't know each other at all. She was certainly qualified, he just wished there had been more time to get to know what really made Bronte tick. He glanced at his wristwatch. There wasn't time. There was never time.

Then perhaps he should make time

Bronte took a breath and waited. She didn't know how long she could keep up this cool act with him towering over her like some feudal warlord—*and one who had pleasured her with the utmost skill.*

Forget that!

Forget that how? Heath's blatant masculinity blazed

in the frame of the intricate graphics framed in his office. He was both an artist and a warrior—and as hard as nails. She could forget those romantic notions she'd been nursing for the past thirteen years. Heath had no intention of softening towards her—towards anything.

'Is it that time already?' he said, glancing at his watch.

Her shoulders slumped. She'd barely been in his office ten minutes. Was that it?

'Shall we go?' he said, staring directly at her.

We? 'Go?' Bronte frowned. 'Go where, Heath?'

'As I told you, I'm running late, and I have an appointment I can't break. We can talk on the way.' He held the door for her.

She let out a tense breath. 'Of course.' It was an unusual interview, but it was an interview.

The Lamborghini was waiting at the steps of Heath's office building. They climbed in and shot away at speed. She couldn't pretend she didn't like Heath's decisive manner or that the electricity between them hadn't increased in the confines of his car. 'Where are we going? she said casually.

'To the launch of one of my games.'

'Great.' Hmm. Okay. Not an interview opportunity—perhaps that would come later, but interesting all the same.

The grand reveal took place in London's most prestigious store. People had been queuing round the block all night in the hope of securing the latest in the long line of hits, and now Heath had explained his premise to her Bronte could understand the enthusiasm that greeted this new game. The little guy putting one over on the bad guys would be a winner every time. And who knew better than Heath about the bad guys? Bronte mused as he escorted her inside the building with a light touch on her arm.

Heath and his team received ear-splitting applause when they took the rostrum. They looked more like a cool rock band than anything else in their motley tops and well worn jeans, fists raised to acknowledge their fans. Heath stayed on to give autographs until Bronte was sure his hand would seize up. He shot her a look halfway through that could be interpreted as: This is my home. This is where I belong—here in London with my team. It was a reminder that the only thing Heath was capable of feeling passion for was his business empire. Sex was a sporting activity like running, or sparring, or working out at the gym—something he enjoyed and was very good at, but realistically sex was only one more way to work off Heath's excess energy.

Which didn't prove to be nearly enough to wipe out how she felt about him.

When the signing was over they said brief goodbyes and Heath escorted her back to the car. She thought he might go back to the office, but their next stop was an upscale restaurant. Good venue to talk, she thought, initially approving Heath's choice. But seeing him again and spending time with him had shaken her up, and she wasn't sure she could relax in such refined surroundings. 'Must we?' She bit her lips, but it was too late.

'Aren't you hungry?' Heath asked. 'I know I am.'

Did Heath's stare have to be quite so direct? 'Well, yes, I am,' she said honestly, finding it impossible to think up an excuse while Heath was raiding her thoughts. She glanced up at the chi-chi sign. Heath had brought her to one of the most famous restaurants in London. 'I don't want you to think I don't appreciate this...'

'But?' he said, angling his chin.

'It's just a little stuffy. I don't know if I could be myself.' As she answered he hit the hazards and left the car. She watched him walk towards the restaurant. Not that Heath walked anywhere—he struts, he strolls, he strides, hummed through her head. Mostly, he moved as he was doing now with that confident, sexy swagger.

But it was a relief not to be entering the hallowed portals, Bronte reflected as Heath disappeared inside. Her emotions were red raw, and she didn't fancy putting them on show for the other diners. She sat forward as Heath breezed out. 'Well?' she demanded as he swung back into the car.

'I cancelled the table.'

'I'm sorry—I hope it wasn't a problem?' Nothing was a problem for Heath, she thought as the Lamborghini roared. 'So where to now?'

'Somewhere I hope you like better—somewhere fun, where you can relax and we can talk.'

'Sounds perfect.' They hadn't done enough of that. But would Heath relax? Glancing across at him, Bronte felt her cheeks burn when Heath caught her staring at him. She could tell he was still buzzing after the signing—still high on adrenalin. She wondered where he'd take her next, and decided to find out—the roundabout way. 'Am I dressed okay for wherever we're going?'

Heath glanced over. 'So long as you think you'll be warm enough.'

'We'll be outside?' She had hinted that she would like to eat somewhere less stuffy than the upmarket restaurant, and there were plenty of hot-dog stands and fast food stalls around London.

'We'll be outside,' Heath confirmed.

'Will I like it?'

'I know I will.'

Heath looked worryingly pleased with himself. She hazarded a guess. 'Why's that? Is there a pool table?'

'Better than that,' Heath said, stopping at the traffic lights.

Okay...

'I hope it isn't too noisy,' she said as the lights turned to green.

'Stop digging, Bronte. It's somewhere you will have to relax—and when you do, maybe we can get a serious discussion going.'

Fun and a serious discussion? How did that work? she wondered, falling silent.

'Still hungry?' Heath demanded, powering away from the traffic lights.

Sadly, for all Bronte's good intentions, she was starving—and not just for food.

CHAPTER ELEVEN

THE Lamborghini sliced through the congested traffic like a well-trained panther, sleek, fast-moving, and effortlessly responsive, while Heath's mind was full of Bronte—the taste of her, her scent, her heat, the way she cried out with pleasure at the moment she let go. It was hard to concentrate with all that running through his head. He made a conscious effort to slow the car, to drive responsibly, to think of Bronte in a purely non-sexual way. He couldn't remember anyone forcing him to look at things and people differently, but Bronte had. He should have known she would follow through with the job—and was glad she had. Bronte had turned out to be by far the best candidate with a wealth of experience, as well as local knowledge second to none. She was right about age having nothing to do with this. Had she been fifty years older he'd still have felt the same.

'Why are you laughing?' she said.

'Nothing,' he said, knowing Bronte had a definite advantage that had nothing to do with professionalism or age. He came up with a suitably distracting reply: 'I was just wondering how you're going to take it when I tell you it will take a while to get where we're going.'

'I think I can hang on,' she said dryly. 'I'm not a baby who needs feeding on the hour.'

'Or rocking to sleep?' he suggested, his mind taking her back to bed again.

'I prefer to keep my eyes open while you're around.'

She was sparking again. That was better. Banter between them was the best cure for tension he knew. Maybe it was time for him to wind down too.

'We'll get there,' she soothed when they got snarled up in a jam.

Driving was partly a distraction, but while they were stuck in traffic like this…

Resting his chin on the back of his hand, he brooded. He could spend the rest of his life living in the past, telling himself he wasn't worthy, but when they were sitting close like this—

'See, we're moving again,' she said just as his thoughts were heating up.

He should have laid everything on the line for her at Hebers Ghyll. He should have told Bronte the type of man he was—the type of man he couldn't be. He should have made that break nice and clean while he'd had the chance—

And then a vehicle swerved in front of them and Bronte exclaimed with fright. He'd avoided it, but it was close. 'You okay?' He reached over to reassure her.

She was staring at his hand on her knee. 'I think so,' she said.

He lifted his hand away. Touching her had fired him. He could only hope the inferno inside him hadn't engulfed the next seat. 'Who chose the outfit?' he said to distract them both.

'Quentin helped me pick it out.'

Traitor, he thought. Quentin was supposed to be his friend. 'You look good.' No harm in telling the truth—

though he put both hands firmly on the wheel. 'Have to say, I pity those sales assistants.'

'Quentin was very polite—and he knows all the best shops,' Bronte protested.

And she's loyal to a fault, he thought. 'I bet he does,' he murmured.

'Quentin was only trying to help, so don't go after him,' Bronte begged him.

'Am I such a monster?' He glanced her way. 'I'm just saying dungarees would have been a better choice for where I'm taking you.'

'I can hardly wait,' she said dryly.

Dipping his head, he scanned the traffic for the quickest way through, making Bronte exclaim a second time when he dropped a gear to overtake some slow-moving vehicles. 'I didn't mean to shake you up.'

'But you have,' she said, giving him the quake with fear routine. 'You're such a scary baddie in your powerful machine, and I'm such a little country innocent all alone in the big city.'

He couldn't have put it better himself.

'So, where are you taking me, Heath?' she probed.

'Like I told you, somewhere fun—somewhere they won't hear you scream when I really give you something to be scared about.'

'Sounds…interesting,' she said, pulling an uncertain face.

'It will be,' he promised.

She shrieked his eardrums out on the big dipper, buried her face in his jacket and clung to him with claws of iron on the Plunge of Doom. She couldn't have done that with anyone else, she assured him, after she'd made him queue for the ride a second time.

'I can't believe you don't know any other adrenalin junkies,' he said, wrapping her in his jacket when she shivered from a combination of freezing wind and her unbounded lust to ride the big wheel.

'I don't know anyone else who would brave my screams a second time,' she said, jumping up and down to keep warm.

The friction at such close range was…interesting. 'I don't mind you screaming, just so long as you don't do it in my ear. The big wheel?'

'Try and keep me off it.

'This was an inspired choice, Heath,' Bronte told him as she marched along, head down against the wind, 'if not exactly what I was expecting as part of my job interview.'

'Performance under stress? Surely, that's a normal part of any interview process?'

'Working for you, I'd say it's an essential part.'

'I aim to please.'

'So screaming might get me brownie points?'

'Screaming will get you all sorts of places, Bronte.' He had the satisfaction of seeing her cheeks glow red.

He gave her his jacket on the big wheel, wondering why he hadn't noticed before how slight she was and how quickly she took cold.

'Are you enjoying it?' she said as the wheel started turning.

'It's a little slow for me,' he admitted, 'though the view is good.' London was unfolding in front of them like one of his fantasy panoramas; a magic carpet in colours of umber and ash, bustling with moving lights beneath a rapidly darkening indigo sky.

'Can you see St Paul's from here?' she said, craning

her neck to look round as their seat reached the highest point.

'I don't know.' He was staring at Bronte when she asked the question.

'Yes,' she cried excitedly. 'Look, Heath—over there.'

Shimmering with light and unwritten stories, the sight of the city would have lifted anyone's mood and Bronte's excitement was infectious. 'I see it.' He sounded as excited as she was.

'This is such an amazing view, isn't it?'

'It's not bad,' he admitted wryly. Bronte's lips were red, her face was flushed and the tip of her pixie nose had turned crimson with cold.

'It's fun, Heath—admit it,' she threatened, doing what he called her bite smile—the big, touching one where the pearly teeth bit down on the full swell of her bottom lip. And this was certainly something. Fun in his world was exploring new markets for his games—checking balance sheets, checking the bank—but Bronte had jolted him out of that perfectly designed world into a realm full of crazy adventure and emotional overspill.

'So you see, you can spare the time,' she told him triumphantly, sitting back against the padded vinyl seat.

'Barely,' he murmured as the wheel began its painfully slow descent.

Bronte's eyes were half shut against the wind, and her face was all screwed up against the biting cold, but even so she was beautiful…and vulnerable, and deserving of someone who would cherish her and focus his whole attention on her—someone who would give Bronte more than he ever could. She shivered again and this time he resisted the temptation to pull her close. Once had been an impulse, twice would make it usual between them, as if they were boyfriend and girlfriend, which they were not.

'What shall we do now?' she said as the wheel stopped to let them get off.

He helped her out. 'What would you like to do?'

'I'll leave that to you—within reason,' she added quickly, shooting him a warning glance. 'And we haven't eaten yet,' she reminded him.

None of this had been planned. It had started out as one thing and ended up as something quite different—the need to talk, the need to get to know each other in the present and find out how they'd changed. The need to do something other than have sex and stalk round each other like two suspicious combatants in the ring. He didn't want to talk about Hebers Ghyll, or business, or Bronte's job. He wanted to do all the things they had never done together, things he'd dreamed about doing with Bronte all those years back—on the rare occasion when he had managed to lift his thoughts above his belt. This was a second chance—a voyage of discovery to find out whether his fantasies had legs.

Guys had fantasies?

Even tough guys like him had fantasies. You want to make something of it? he challenged his inner voice.

'Brrh, it's cold,' Bronte said, shrinking deeper into his giant-sized jacket.

'How about somewhere warm now?' he suggested.

'You read my mind.' She laughed up at him. 'Are you going to tell me where, or are you going to keep me hanging?'

'I'm going to take you to see a small corner of my world.'

'Will I need lifts in my shoes?'

He glanced down at her flats and laughed. 'I'll make sure no one treads on you.'

Bronte laughed. And now they were both laughing. And before he knew what he was doing he'd dragged her close.

She hugged him hard. They broke away as if they both knew it was wrong, and could only lead them down the same blind alley. There was a certain amount of awkwardness between them until he said, 'Can you dance?'

Her face lit up. 'What do you think, rubber legs? But I thought we were going somewhere to eat first.'

'We are. Come on,' he said, urging her towards the car.

'You're not taking me somewhere stuffy like that last place, are you?' she said, looking up at him.

He liked she'd got her confidence back. He was not quite so pleased when she raced ahead of him and started scampering backwards. He'd been down that road too many times. 'Wait and see,' he said, gathering her under his arm before they repeated their signature move.

'Okay,' she said, staring up at him as they strode along purposefully, side by side, keeping in step. 'This sounds mysterious. Are you going to give me any clues?'

'No.'

And with that she had to be content.

Why wouldn't Heath tell her where they were going? Another small corner of his world, he'd said. Today was turning out to be like a jigsaw someone had tossed up in the air. Find the right pieces and you might see the picture clearly. But she liked a mystery. And she liked what she'd seen so far.

Had she never dreamed that Heath was human?

Bronte wondered, snuggling deeper into his jacket while he drove them to another part of the city. Heath had shown another side of himself tonight, and it was a side that she liked—a side that tempted her to forget all her warnings to self about not getting in any deeper than she already had. She jerked alert and looked around as he pulled the Lamborghini off the road and killed the engine. 'You're kidding me?' she exclaimed softly as she peered out of the window. Of all the possible destinations, this was the very last place on earth she would have connected with the hard man at her side. A retro café complete with pink neon signs and garish orange paintwork. 'You're not short on surprises, Heath.'

'I have connections here,' he explained, only adding to the mystery. 'Maybe it's a little crazy.'

'Lucky for you,' Bronte admitted with a grin. 'I love crazy.'

Heath was one complex guy, Bronte thought as he opened the car door for her.

'I trust this fits your brief for something different?' Heath said, making her a mock bow as he helped her out of the car.

'I can't even imagine how you come to know about a place like this,' she said, staring wide-eyed at the clientele flooding in.

'My friend owns it,' Heath explained.

'Cool…I can't wait to see inside.' Though she was definitely underdressed for this gig. The girls she was following into the café were dressed in fifties outfits— high ponytails and bright red lipstick, their short flared skirts held out by yards of stiff net petticoats. They wore short white socks with high-heeled shoes, and wide, brightly coloured belts to emphasise their waists, while the men were boasting velvet-collared suits and winkle-picker shoes.

'You do jive, I take it?' Heath said dryly as he handed over the entrance fee for both of them.

She frowned—and, only half joking, asked, 'Is this part of my job interview?'

'You should know. You have to be quick on your feet on a farm.'

Bronte shook her head. 'I guess I jive, then.' She'd just have to get the hang of it in a hurry.

'Great—then, let's go,' Heath said, brandishing their tickets.

This certainly wasn't the man she thought she knew. Heath had more facets than a hard black diamond and kept most of them under wraps. She was surprised he was sharing this much with her.

Once bitten, Bronte reminded herself when she felt Heath's hand come to rest in the small of her back as he guided her safely through the crowd. That touch was a timely, if unwelcome reminder that having fun together was one thing, but having sex—well, that was a whole world of difference. Fun she could bank and smile about when she got back to work. Sex was something you didn't have with the boss—something that tore at your heart and left it in pieces.

So why melt? Why long? Why ache? Why do any of those things? Take the evening for what it was, and then get on with your life, Bronte told herself firmly, glancing around with interest and anticipation.

The beat was pounding inside an interior that faithfully recreated an authentic fifties coffee bar. There was a black and white tiled floor, Formica tables with lots of chrome around, and padded banquettes, covered in shiny red plastic that didn't even pretend to be leather, and the most fantastic burnished wood panelling. 'Carved by a regular customer,' Heath said, pointing it out. He went on to explain that the café had recently been made a listed building, which meant it was destined to be preserved just as it was. He'd barely had chance to give her this potted history when a good-looking man spotted him and came over. 'Heath—long time.'

As the two men shared a man hug Bronte wondered about the connection between them.

'Josh,' Heath said, introducing his friend to Bronte. 'Josh and I—we spent some time together when we were younger.'

No further explanations necessary, Bronte thought as Josh shook her hand. Josh was another bad boy made good.

'I haven't seen Heath for ages—you must be good for him,' Josh said, an attractive crease appearing in his face as he searched out a table for them.

'I think you'll like the food here,' Heath confided, dipping his head down to shout in Bronte's ear above the music. He was guiding her through the danger zone of spinning couples to take the booth Josh had indicated. 'It's all home-cooking. Josh's mother is in the kitchen making pasta, pies, bread pudding and custard, jam roly-poly—you name it.'

'Fattening?' she suggested wryly.

'Delicious,' Heath argued firmly with a smile that lit a bonfire in her heart.

It was a revelation to discover Heath's world wasn't the soulless vacuum of cyberspace she'd imagined, but something far more diverse and interesting. And he was loyal too—something she had already seen in his relationship with Quentin. So the lone wolf did have friends. It made her optimistic, somehow—

Irrelevant, Bronte told herself firmly as Heath sat down across the plastic table from her. This was a… business meeting? Heath's stare was disturbingly direct. What did he expect her to say or do? She felt uncertain suddenly.

And her heart?

Didn't stand a chance faced by this new understanding growing between them.

Friendship, Bronte thought as Heath handed her the menu. This was friendship growing between them, and that was…that was nice.

'Relax, Bronte—just choose something to eat and forget about everything else.'

Sure. She could do that. Wasn't living for the moment her speciality? Forget those thirteen years of longing, the trial relationships with other men—failures all of them, because all she had ever done was compare them with Heath, so every man had fallen short.

So here she was again, back on that same old roller coaster, Bronte reflected—all that was missing was a platter on which to serve herself up—

No. No! *No!* Being here with Heath didn't mean she was going to have sex with him. It wasn't compulsory. It didn't come with the bill. They were having a meal together. What was wrong with that?

She selected home-made cannelloni with spinach and ricotta and a tomato juice with the works to drink. Heath chose steak and chips, and a beer. 'Dance while we wait for the food?' he suggested with a glance at the whirling couples.

She drew a steadying breath before answering. Dancing was a kind of intimacy—there weren't too many things a man and woman could do together in rhythm—

Hey…lighten up, she told herself, glancing down at her flat shoes. 'Are you serious?' She wanted to dance, really. It would be fun. She couldn't jive, but what the heck?

'Those shoes are perfect,' Heath observed. 'Anyone would think you knew you were coming here. Think of the steps you can do in those.'

'I have thought,' she assured him dryly. 'And we both know my sense of balance isn't up to much.'

'It doesn't have to be,' Heath said, 'as I'm here to catch you.' Standing up, he made it hard for Bronte to refuse.

'I can't…I really can't,' she said, changing her mind. How could she when her heart was going wild at the thought of dancing with Heath?

'I'm not taking no for an answer,' he said. And when she still hung back, he grabbed her hand. 'I never took you for a chicken, Ms Foster-Jenkins.'

'Squawk squawk.'

'You can move your hips, can't you?'

Who knew that better than Heath? Standing hands on hips waiting for her to cave, Heath looked hot enough to fry a steak on. But this could end really badly, Bronte reasoned. Letting herself go with Heath was hardly sensible: hot, hectic movements—Heath's firm hands directing her—staring into each other's eyes— Hmm. When had she done that before?

And there was another issue. Most men couldn't dance. Could Heath dance? Or would she soon be running for the exit?

Heath could dance. Why was she surprised? Heath was so brazenly male, so relentlessly sexy, he could make any move look cool—something that wasn't lost on the women gathered round him. And he taught her to jive in the same effortless way in which he'd taught her to make love. And then the DJ changed the track and Heath's mouth curved in a challenging grin.

'Twist contest?' Bronte asked, eyes widening in trepidation.

'We have to,' he said, kicking off his loafers. 'And we have to do this right.'

She should have known Heath could out-dance a movie star and look hotter than hell. The crowd grew around him and somehow she forgot her good intentions again. Staring into Heath's eyes, she really went for it, while Heath's body brushed hers into a state of arousal.

Lucky for her, their food was delivered to the table or she'd have been right back where she started from, Bronte thought. Much safer to have Heath call it a day and escort her back to the table.

But with Heath's hand back home in the small of her back she couldn't help wondering who was kidding who here.

CHAPTER TWELVE

THE food was delicious and Bronte ate ravenously. It was easy to talk about Hebers Ghyll in such a relaxed setting, though she prickled all over when Heath admitted he still couldn't see how the inheritance would fit into his life. She could see the problem. Heath's life was cool and cutting edge. Hebers Ghyll was a lumbering great piece of real estate with thousands of acres of land attached. But it was somewhere she called home. She couldn't expect it to be more than another entry in Heath's property portfolio. She had to make him see it differently. If she could only persuade him to come back.

'Don't let your food get cold,' Heath advised when she started out down that route.

Heath would never be pushed. And she would not be moved. Things promised to get interesting. They already were; Heath was close enough for her body to warm at the memory of his touch—

'Penny for them?' he murmured.

Censored. 'Just thinking what a really great time I've had tonight.'

'I'll call for the bill.'

She dug out her purse.

'Put that away.'

Resolutions were easy to make, but the warmth and

strength of Heath's hand covering hers was too much. She snatched her hand away as if he'd burned it. 'I can't let you pay for me, Heath.'

'Then take it as wages. I must owe you something by now?'

'Yes, you do,' she said frankly, 'but this is different—separate.'

'Then you'll just have to repay me some other way.' Heath curved a smile. 'I'm sure I can find some filing for you at the office, if you're really desperate?'

'Temping for you?' she said. 'I don't think so.'

'You're probably right,' Heath agreed, 'I'd get no work done by the time you'd finished tempting—'

'Temping,' she corrected him. 'You mean when I've finished temping.'

'You say temping—I say tempting.' Heath's cheek creased in a grin.

Heath was enjoying himself. The revelation made her thrill inside. 'You're impossible,' she scolded him.

'I know,' he agreed, putting his hand up for the bill.

They went from the heat of the café into the cool of the night. Heath opened the passenger door of the Lamborghini and Bronte fed herself in.

'You're getting better at it,' he observed dryly.

'And you're not supposed to be looking.'

'I'll try to remember that.'

She doubted he would. And if it was possible to enter such a low-slung car without showing everything she was born with and a whole lot more, she hadn't got the knack of it yet.

'So where now?' she asked as Heath swung in beside her.

Self-doubt crowded in when Heath said nothing. Having sex with him would be spectacular—but wrong. It would be the perfect ending to the perfect night, but that didn't make it right. It was everything she had promised herself she wouldn't do. 'We'll find a hotel as we drive back to town—you can just drop me—'

'Let you loose on the unsuspecting?' Heath said, gunning the engine. 'I couldn't be so unfeeling towards my fellow man.'

'Look,' she said a few miles further down the road, 'that looks like a nice bed and breakfast. You can drop me here. It says vacancies—I'll be fine.'

More silence.

'Heath?' she prompted as he started to make a call. She couldn't risk everything she'd dreamed about and worked towards, sacrificed for a night that would leave her heart in pieces. 'Heath, what are you doing?' She felt the prickle of apprehension creep up her spine as Heath held up his hand to silence her, and as the conversation got under way she felt sick. The bottom dropped out of her world when she realised Heath was booking a double room at some swanky hotel in Knightsbridge. She was supposed to be grateful, Bronte guessed. And why should Heath think any differently of her? She'd had sex with him and enjoyed it—they'd both enjoyed it. She would be the first to admit she wanted him more than ever. But not like this.

'Yes,' Heath confirmed. 'An executive double for tonight.' He paused and flashed a glance at Bronte as the girl on the other end of the line obviously checked her reservation system. Once the booking was confirmed, he added, 'We'll be with you in around a quarter of an hour.'

'What are you doing?' Bronte whispered the moment

Heath cut the line. Had the wonderful time they had spent together been for this? Was the friendship she thought they had forged nothing more than an illusion?

'Lucky they had a room available.'

And she was available too? Bronte thought dully, turning to stare out of the window. This would ruin everything.

Her anxiety had reached epic proportions by the time Heath pulled into the approach of one of the most famous five-star hotels in London. She had to hand it to him, when it came to seduction Heath didn't stint.

'I know the staff here,' he explained as a uniformed valet approached the car and took his keys through the open window.

Of course he did. Where wouldn't Heath be known? Bronte wondered.

'They'll make you welcome, and you'll be safe here.'

Safe with Heath?

He was at her side of the car opening the door before the porter even had chance to react. 'Come on.' He held out his hand. 'I'll cover for you.'

He could still joke about this? She held back. Heath was waiting. The porter was staring. 'I don't have any luggage. What will people think?'

'Since when have you cared?' Heath lifted her out and deposited her on the pavement in front of him, holding her shoulders so he could stare into her eyes. 'I don't care what people think and neither should you. Where are you going now?' he said, catching hold of her wrist.

'I'll take a cab.'

'A cab where? Don't be ridiculous, Bronte.'

A well dressed couple made a point of skirting round them.

'It's only a bed for the night.'

'I don't know how you can say that.'

Heath thumbed his chin, and then he started to laugh.

'Did I say something funny?' Bronte snapped.

'What kind of man do you think I am, Bronte? Did you really think I'd let you take pot luck where you slept tonight?'

'I thought—'

'I know what you thought,' Heath said, losing the smile. 'I'm getting your signals loud and clear. Perhaps now is a good time to tell you that I've never had to engineer an opportunity for sex, and I'm sure as hell not starting now.'

'But you booked a double room,' Bronte challenged heatedly.

'Single rooms are too small—usually by the elevator, and always my last choice. I got you an executive double, the cost of which,' he assured her, 'I will knock off your wages. But as for sleeping with you, Bronte?' Turning, Heath pointed across the road. 'My house is right over there. Why would I want to stay with you?'

For no reason she could think of.

'You thought I'd booked a double room so we could have sex?' Heath's face was a mask of exasperation and disappointment.

'Well, excuse me for getting the wrong end of the stick,' Bronte fired back.

They were standing toe to toe when Heath shook his head and said icily, 'See you back at Hebers Ghyll?'

His meaning was clear. 'So for a misunderstanding I lose the job?' She was so far down the road she couldn't find her way back and was half out of her mind with panic and frustration.

'No,' Heath countered. 'For always thinking the worst of me you lose the job. How could you work for a boss you don't trust, Bronte? Well, could you?' And when she didn't answer, Heath raged, 'Do you know what?' His hair was sticking up in angry spikes where he'd raked it. 'I used to think I was the one stuck in the past, but now I see it's you, Bronte. You just can't let go of who I used to be. You've kept those thoughts alive for all these years—thinking tough is good and hard is sexy. Well, here's some news for you. I don't want to be that man—and I especially don't want to be that man with you.'

She looked at Heath open-mouthed. If only half what he said was true then she was bitterly ashamed. They changed each other, Bronte realised as she sucked in a shuddering breath. They brought out the best and the worst in each other. 'Heath—' she reached out to him '—please, I—'

Heath pulled away as if she had the plague. 'Stay or don't stay—I really don't care what you do. The room's paid for,' he rapped. 'Have it on me.' And with that he spun on his heel and strode away.

Wound up like a spring, she watched him, and stood rooted to that same spot until she heard the engine roar and saw the Lamborghini speed away.

It was a much subdued Bronte who followed the house-keeper to her room. In her current bewildered state it was much better to stay put, she had concluded. After all, she had nowhere else to go. Her guilt doubled and doubled again when she was shown into the most sump-tuous double room—*well away from the elevators.*

Sumptuously decorated in shades of aquamarine, ivory and coral, with ornate plasterwork on the ceiling playing host to a glittering chandelier, it was a mocking reminder that she wasn't always right, and that sometimes she was horribly wrong. She stood in the centre of the room when the housekeeper left her, inhaling the scent of fresh flowers from the market, beautifully arranged in a crystal bowl on the dressing table. If she had taken that bowl and smashed it she couldn't have done more harm tonight. She had taken something beautiful and twisted it with her suspicion. She had killed any hope of Heath being a friend, and a friend was something more than a lover—something less than both, but something precious all the same.

Lying on the bed fully clothed she ran through the evening in her head. What had Heath done wrong—other than his crazy driving and his insistence that she had to eat roly-poly pudding or he couldn't eat his?

Turning her face into the pillow, she was crying as she made an angry sound of frustration. She would go to any lengths not to hurt him—and had failed spectacularly. She had allowed her own insecurities to spill out in reproach and accusation. Why couldn't she just accept that Heath had wanted to do something nice for her? Was he always going to be the bad boy in her eyes? The fact he'd worked that out for himself made her clutch the pillow tighter. Heath had grown beyond his past, and he was right—she was the one who had refused to see it.

Rolling her head on the pillows, she refused to cry any more. She squeezed her eyes shut, welcoming the darkness. It was warm and soft, and short on condemnation, and with that and the lavender-scented pillows to lull her ragged senses she drifted off to sleep.

She woke up with a start an hour or so later. At first

she didn't know where she was—until she took in the huge bed, the crisp white linen and the rest of her surroundings, along with the fact that she was fully dressed. She was in a hotel—a very fancy hotel. Her room was sumptuous, but impersonal, as all such rooms were. The feeling that struck her next was loneliness. Hugging herself, she crossed to the window and stared out. Heath had said his house was just across the road...

Heath wouldn't be standing by his window staring out, Bronte reasoned turning away with a shrug. Heath would have more sense.

He was pacing. He couldn't stand inactivity and liked indecision even less. He hated the fact that the evening had ended on a row, and that the friction between them had increased, sending everything up in the air again, leaving everything unfinished. Before the row they had been drawing closer, getting to know each other all over again, but after it— He snapped a glance out of the window at the hotel where Bronte was staying. He had chosen a hotel most convenient to him—most convenient if things went well and if they went badly.

Bronte touched him in ways no one else had ever done, brought another side of him into existence—a side he had kept buried for most, if not all of his adult life. Emotions, inconvenient and dangerously distracting. He buried them. Bronte rooted them out, forcing him to confront his feelings and challenging his famous self-control.

And what had he done for Bronte?

He had made her face reality instead of blurring the lines between that and the fantasies she liked to weave.

So what was he saying? They completed each other?

He had thought the only thing that could touch him was business, but if those weren't feelings they'd been expressing tonight, he didn't know what they were. And if Bronte's face hadn't reflected her shock when she realised there was more to this association of theirs than pick-and-mix dreams, then that big dose of reality really had passed her by.

Turning back to his desk, he fingered the contract he'd had drawn up by his lawyers, itemizing the formal conditions for a six-month trial of the new estate manager at Hebers Ghyll. It was something he had intended to raise with Bronte, but they had both needed cooling-down time, and space from each other so they could rejig their thoughts. Bronte would leave London tomorrow. She was safer in the country—safe in the city too, so long as he stayed away. Tomorrow would be different. Tomorrow it would be all about business.

She took a long, warm bath, trying to convince herself that because this was such luxury it would somehow soothe her. It meant nothing. She would rather have slept on a park bench and remained friends with Heath than lie here in scented foam in the fabulous suite of rooms Heath had paid for because he wanted to keep her safe—because Heath had wanted to give her something nice, a treat, only for her to throw it back in his face. She'd get up early and go home, Bronte reflected as she climbed out and grabbed a towel. She could only wait and see if Heath's personal feelings would negate the grilling he'd managed to slip in while they were both relaxed enough to talk frankly to each other during their crazy fun day out.

'That was quite some interviewing technique, mister,'

she murmured wistfully, gazing at her shadowy reflection in the mirror on the wall. The suite was sumptuous, but the lights were cruel. Or maybe she had just aged. More likely, she'd had a shocking hold-the-mirror-up-to-yourself moment, and grown up.

All of the above, Bronte concluded.

She turned at a knock on the door.

Heath?

Heath was her first—her only thought.

Her heart was racing by the time she'd grabbed a robe and raced out of the bathroom, across the bedroom, to throw the lock, and opened the door.

On an empty corridor.

Glancing up and down, conscious she wasn't dressed for public display, she retreated quickly and pressed the door to again, locking it securely. It was only when she calmed down she saw the note on the floor. Express check-out details?

It had to be...

But they wouldn't call her Bronte, would they? The hotel wouldn't write that on the front of the envelope in bold script, using a fountain pen.

She ripped the envelope apart and let it fall to the floor. Unfolding the single sheet of high quality notepaper, she read the brief message. Heath would like to see her in the morning, before she returned to the country...9 a.m., his house.

She scanned the letter again. It was more of a note—no flourishes, no personal asides, just Heath's London address printed in raised script on the top right-hand corner. It was yet another kick-in-the-teeth reminder that Heath was in another place from the boy who had loved nothing more than a rough-house behind the stables with anyone foolish enough to take him on. Heath was a self-educated gentleman of culture and means these days, and it was Bronte who needed to get her head out of the sand.

CHAPTER THIRTEEN

THE outside of Heath's town house was a paean to elegance. Palladian pillars framed neatly trimmed bay trees either side of an imposing front door. The dark blue paintwork was so flawless it had the appearance of sapphire glass. The door knocker was a gleaming lion with bared teeth.

How appropriate, Bronte thought as her hand hovered over it. She was bang on time. She had made sure of it. As she waited on the neat, square mat she noticed the matching door knob was a smooth, tactile globe that would fit Heath's hand perfectly. Imagining his hand closed around it, she drew a sharp breath as he opened the door.

'Welcome to my home.' Heath, tall, dark and frighteningly charismatic, held the door open for her.

There was nothing to suggest he bore a grudge, or that last night had been the blitz of emotions she remembered. Heath was all business this morning. 'Thank you.' She stepped past his powerful presence into the hall.

Having left the crisp air of early morning behind only one thought hit her and that was, Wow. The warmth and luxury of Heath's home enveloped her immediately, as did the restrained décor in shades of cream, white, beige and ivory—the occasional blast of colour provided by vivid works of art hanging on flawless, chalky-white walls.

Everything was spotless, and in its place—but this wasn't just a showpiece, she realised, gazing around, this was a home. A bolt of longing grabbed her when she took in all the personal touches. They were in an imposing square hall tiled in black and white marble. The lofty ceiling was decorated with beautifully restored plasterwork, and the doors were heavy, polished wood. How had she missed so much about Heath? She must have been wearing blinkers. Yes, he was the same warrior, as evidenced by his business prowess now, but he was a protector too, as she knew from his care of her in London, and he was fun and sexy, clever—and could be a regular pain in the neck, when he put his mind to it, she thought, smiling to herself as Heath drew her deeper into the house. And the more she saw, the more she realised she had imagined many things over the years about Heath, but she had never pictured him as a homemaker. There was mail waiting to be posted on the antique console table with the gilt-framed mirror over it, as well as a couple of recently delivered yachting magazines, still in their cellophane wrappers. There was even a high-tech racing bike propped beside the front door—

'Bronte?' Heath prompted.

She was turning full circle like a tourist at the Louvre, Bronte realised—probably with her mouth wide open. How rude! Red-cheeked, she followed Heath down the hallway. She spied a litter of books scattered across a squashy sofa through one open door—his living room, she presumed. Classical music was playing softly in the background, and a log fire was murmuring in the hearth. He must have been relaxing there, waiting for her to arrive.

Nice to know someone could relax, she thought wryly as they passed another door. This opened onto a cloak-room with a boot rack stacked with an assortment of footwear and rugged jackets slung on antique hooks. It was all rather bloke-ish, and yet reassuringly normal for such a wealthy man.

And welcoming. That was her overriding impression, Bronte realised. Whether Heath knew it or not he had absorbed everything Uncle Harry had created at Hebers Ghyll. This was a real home, where the original features of the house had been retained and married with practi-cality and luxury, she thought as Heath showed her into his study. Understated and original were the keynotes that distinguished Heath's home—but then he was an artist too, she remembered. If Heath could be persuaded to work this type of magic on Hebers Ghyll, the estate really would live again.

And their friendship? What were the odds on that surviving? Bronte wondered as Heath invited her to take a seat on the opposite side of his desk. There was noth-ing intimate in his tone of voice. It was all business for him now.

'You know what this is?' he said, pushing a sheaf of documents towards her.

She looked at him—looked into Heath's deep, com-plex gaze. It sucked her in…and left her floundering. 'A contract?' she said, quickly gathering her scattered thoughts.

'It's a legal document setting out the terms for a six-month trial. Read it, and if you agree it, sign it.' Uncapping the same fountain pen with which he must have written the brief note inviting her to his London home, he handed it to her. 'I'll leave you while you read and consider—and you don't have to sign anything right away. You don't have to sign it at all.'

'But—' She stood, wanting to thank him. This was everything she had ever dreamed of. And how flat dreams could feel when they came true, she thought as Heath left the room.

But this wasn't just about her. There were others she had to think about. She sat down again and started to read, but all the time she was aware of the lovingly polished wood around her, and the warm, clean air, lightly fragranced with Heath's shower soap—

Heath...

She'd pushed him away, shaking her head as if that could rid it of him—and was left with a contract.

He'd had a breakfast meeting with the lawyers to get the contract finalised—except he hadn't eaten breakfast, and now he was hungry. He glanced at the cooker and the fridge—glanced at his wristwatch and thought of Bronte. He wanted her to be secure. He'd given her a cast-iron contract that protected her and gave her a pay-out if she changed her mind about working on the estate.

'I can't sign this, Heath.'

He turned to see her framed in the doorway. 'Can't or won't?' he said coolly.

'You know what's in here. It isn't fair.'

'No?' His lips pressed down in a rueful smile as she walked across the room. 'I thought it was very fair.'

'But there's nothing in it for you—no guarantees for you.'

'It's six months, Bronte.' He shrugged. 'You tell me how much I stand to lose.'

'You stand to lose a lot,' she insisted, coming close to make her point. 'You know you do, Heath.'

'Do I?' As Bronte's clean, wildflower scent invaded his senses he felt less than nothing about his losses—which was a first for him in business, he registered with wryly.

'Look at this clause, as an example,' she said, showing him the relevant passage. 'This is ridiculous—I don't need special treatment.'

'Do you find it patronising?' Heath asked as she turned her face up to him.

'Well, yes, I do, actually,' she said. 'Would anyone else get this sort of contract? I doubt it, Heath.'

'Does friendship count for nothing, Bronte?'

'Friendship...' She looked at him in something close to bewilderment.

Leaning back against the counter, he was acutely conscious of Bronte standing only inches away. 'Sign or don't sign,' he said, shifting position and moving away.

'I want to be the best person for the job, Heath.' She frowned. 'But you don't seem to care what I do, which doesn't fill me with confidence. I don't want any special favours. I want you to take me on because I'm the best.'

'You are the best candidate,' he said evenly, meeting her gaze.

'And the rest of it?' she said.

He stared away into his thoughts. 'I just want you to be happy, Bronte. It's all I've ever wanted.'

How could she be? Bronte wondered as her fingers closed around the contract. Heath was right, this contract had been her goal, but wanting Heath eclipsed everything, which meant this piece of paper with its more than generous terms fell so far short of what she had hoped for, she could hardly raise the energy to sign it.

'I'm not changing a word of it,' Heath told her. 'But I will give you a little more time to decide if you want to go ahead and sign it. In the meantime—' his lips tugged up in a faint smile '—have you eaten anything this morning?'

'No…have you?'

Their gazes held for a moment. If this was friend-ship—this feeling that survived everything—then she'd take it.

'Are you hungry, Bronte?'

Heath's question made her nose sting. 'I'm hungry,' she said.

'Then let's go into the kitchen and I'll make you something to eat.'

'You cook?'

'I cook,' Heath confirmed.

He led the way into a large, airy kitchen. With its glass roof, and fabulous state-of-the-art appliances, it had the spacious feel of an orangerie. 'Did you design it?' she said, looking around.

'I prepared the brief, did the drawings, and sourced the materials, so there could be no mistakes,' Heath ex-plained, reaching for a pan and turning on the cooker.

'Did you do most of the work yourself?' she said, admiring the way the original ornate plasterwork had been incorporated into the modern design.

'Most of it—though I did allow the interior designers to plump the cushions when I'd finished.'

When Heath curved a smile it was like a light turning on, Bronte thought, but she mustn't be dazzled by it.

'Eggs Benedict?'

'Are you serious?'

'Absolutely. I like eating—so it's essential that I cook.'

She laughed, and finally relaxed.

He loved the sound of Bronte laughing. It was the only soundtrack he needed. He found a bowl and started whisking. 'Why don't you sit and read your contract? This will take a few minutes.'

As Heath got busy cracking eggs and reaching for the seasoning she laid the contract on the cool black granite, and signed it without another word.

Tipping buttery sauce onto the spinach, eggs and muffins, he came to sit next to her at the breakfast bar. 'You signed it,' he said, brow furrowing as he stared at the contract.

'And here's your copy,' she said, handing him half the papers. 'Eat. You must be hungry too. This is delicious, Heath,' she commented after the first mouthful.

Their arms were almost touching. This was the closest they had come to relaxing together since—since she didn't want to think about. She wanted to start over—this way—with a friendship between two adults—just see where it led. Nowhere, probably, but, hey—

'Now you're formally part of the team,' Heath said as he forked up egg, 'I'll tell you my thoughts about Hebers Ghyll.' Was that disappointment in Bronte's eyes? Wasn't this what she wanted? 'If there's something else you'd like to discuss first?'

'Nothing,' she protested, a little too vigorously, he thought. 'I'd like to hear your plans, Heath.'

'Okay.' As he talked he wondered if she was listening. She looked intent, but she was looking *at* him rather than listening to what he was telling her. It could wait, he thought, starting to collect the plates up.

'Is that it?' she said.

'For now.'

'So you started off thinking, "What do I need this for?" when you inherited,' she guessed, 'and then found me camped out on your latest acquisition and discovered a sense of ownership.'

A grin creased his face. 'That's pretty much the version I remember.'

'At least by camping out I got your interest.'

'You got something,' Heath agreed as they filled the dishwasher together, arms brushing, faces close. 'And your campaign won through,' he admitted tongue in cheek. 'I'm going to keep the place, aren't I?' he said, straightening up. 'And I want you to have the pleasure of telling everyone their jobs are safe.'

Her face brightened in a quick smile—a smile she found hard to sustain and so she turned away from him.

Everything would be all right now, Bronte told herself firmly. Heath would have to come down to visit. His visits would be formal affairs—but they'd be visits.

'I thought I might open part of the house and grounds to the public.'

She turned. 'But that's a wonderful idea.'

'It makes a certain amount of sense,' Heath agreed.

As always, he was the one under control. 'It makes more than sense,' she couldn't stop herself exclaiming. 'Uncle Harry would have loved that idea—'

'What you have to understand,' Heath interrupted, 'is that I own the estate now, Bronte.'

'Of course I realise that—I do,' she assured him, struggling to rein back her emotions. 'And anything you want me to do when I go back—just add it to the list.' She was ready to start work right away—this minute—but the look Heath was giving her was different from the way she felt inside. It was steadier—brooding, almost. 'What?' she said.

Heath's powerful shoulders eased in a shrug. 'I've been thinking that maybe I'll open an office there.'

Thank you, thank you...

Bronte's lips pressed down in a good imitation of, okay, then—no big deal. And then Heath got into practical matters—bricks and mortar, balance sheets, and making the place pay for itself, while she told him everything she could remember that made Hebers Ghyll so special to her. All the little things that had coloured her childhood, like the lush tang of newly mown meadow grass—eating hazelnuts straight from the bush, if the squirrels hadn't got to them first—blackthorn bushes heavy with purple sloe—

'Do you remember that sloe gin we made?' Heath interrupted.

'Do I remember it? I remember how sick we were after we drank it.'

'And then your mother threw it down the sink,' Heath said, laughing. 'She probably saved our lives.'

'Almost certainly...'

Bronte fell silent as a pang of regret swept over her. She missed her parents and wished she'd had the opportunity to tell them how much she loved them, and what a happy childhood they'd given her, before they left. She'd call them the first chance she got and make sure they knew. She had taken so much for granted, Bronte realised now this chance to see life through Heath's eyes reminded her that he had enjoyed none of her benefits, and yet had always looked to the future with optimism and confidence, while she had been restless and dissatisfied when she had so much. 'Your turn,' she said, prompting him. 'What else do you remember?' She grimaced as soon as the words left her mouth, thinking about Heath's difficult youth. 'Sorry—I didn't mean—'

'Hey—get over it. I have,' Heath said. 'Fun?' He thought about it for a moment. 'Sorting out this place.' He glanced around. 'It was a dump when I bought it. It was the only way I could afford something in central London—'

And then he started to tell her about the city he had grown to love with its galleries and museums, and the ancient buildings he loved to visit that had whetted his appetite for preservation and restoration. 'I enjoy the concerts too.'

'You like music?'

'Jazz, rock, classics—of course I like music. What?' he demanded when Bronte seemed surprised. 'Do you think I spend all my time working out and eating nails for breakfast?'

'Don't you?'

He laughed.

'And what about Hebers Ghyll, Heath? What good things do you remember about your visits?'

'Your mother's cooking,' he said immediately. 'Hot meals—Uncle Harry teaching me chess...' He fell silent.

'I'm sure Uncle Harry enjoyed those visits as much as you did.'

'We had a—' Heath pulled a face '—let's just call it a pretty explosive relationship, but chess was our meeting ground. The game was all about tactics, Uncle Harry said. He told me that whatever happened to me in my life, I would always need to use tactics—so I'd better get my head around them whether I liked chess or not.'

'That sounds like Uncle Harry,' Bronte said, smiling as she remembered. 'And did you?'

'Did I what?'

Heath was gazing at her lips. 'Did you like the game?' she said, wiping them surreptitiously in case some of their breakfast spinach was still hanging around.

'I like the game,' Heath said, transferring his level gaze to her eyes.

What were they talking about now? Tingles ran down her spine.

'Would you like me to complete the guided tour?' Heath suggested, stretching his powerful limbs as if the inactivity was starting to get to him.

'I'd like that very much,' she said.

CHAPTER FOURTEEN

THEY left the kitchen and walked deeper into the house, crossing wonderful rugs in shades of marmalade, clotted cream and russet that softened the marble hall and gave the space an inviting glow. Heath had created something wonderful and she guessed he must have dreamed of living in a house like this when he was a boy. Heath had not only fulfilled those dreams, but had done so with his own hands, which must have been doubly rewarding for him. There was a wood-panelled library where a worn leather chesterfield sat on a faded Persian rug and a log fire blazed in the hearth, as well as a high-tech studio where Heath could work. 'And below us in the basement I've got a cinema room, a home gym, and an indoor swimming pool,' he explained.

'Of course you have,' she teased him, but this was all seriously fabulous, even for such an upscale area of the city.

'Upstairs?' he suggested.

'Why not?' With this new understanding between them, why should there be any no-go areas?

They were easy together. They were going to have a good working relationship, Bronte thought as she followed Heath up the stairs. They'd had their explosion, their resolution, and now they were starting afresh.

Heath was so athletic she had to run to keep up with him, though he barely seemed to exert himself as he sprinted up the beautifully restored central staircase. 'The bathroom,' he said, opening one of the doors with a flourish.

She was still admiring the light-drenched landing. 'You are kidding me?' She stood on the threshold of the bathroom, staring in. 'This is fantastic, Heath.' The bathroom was clad in black marble and brightened with mirrors. There was a huge, walk-in drench shower, with a spa bath big enough to swim in. 'And I bet the floor is heated.' She kicked off her shoes. 'It is.'

'You don't exactly go down to the lake to freshen up.'

'Maybe not—but I know where to look when I need a refit.'

'It will cost you.'

She tore her gaze away when it held and locked with Heath's. Heath was at his most feral and the dream-weaver was back, and wouldn't take no for an answer, so when she should have left the room and allowed Heath to continue on with his tour she leaned back against the door, trapping them both on the bathroom side.

'Stop it,' Heath warned in an undertone, but then his lips tugged in a teasing smile. 'Don't you have a train to catch?'

'Yes,' she admitted. What was she thinking? She pulled away from the door, and Heath, ever the gentleman, leaned across to open it for her. Their bodies brushed. Electricity fired. This wasn't meant to happen—

'No,' he said, as if responding to her. 'No, Bronte,' he said more firmly.

Her eyes searched his.

'I'm no good for you,' he said.

She closed her eyes and inhaled sharply. 'And I'm stuck in the past? Stop it—stop it now, Heath.' Some primal instinct made her lift her arm and put her hand across his mouth. 'I don't want to hear that ever again,' she said.

Heath's eyes were laughing as his tongue went on the attack—tickling, and licking—

'Stop it,' she warned him, whipping her hand away.

'You stop it,' Heath said, laughing.

She exclaimed as he dragged her into his arms. 'What do you think you're doing?' she demanded as he swept her off her feet and headed for the drench shower. 'No!' she screamed when Heath's intention became clear.

'I need to cool you down,' he said. 'And if words won't do it—'

She watched him turn the shower to the coldest setting and screamed again, but it was pointless fighting Heath. And now he was under the water with her, holding her in place with embarrassing ease. 'Have you had enough yet?' he said, holding her in front of him.

They were both soaked through. 'What do you think?' She couldn't even pretend to be angry. Flicking her hair out of her eyes, she started laughing, and once she'd started she couldn't stop. Then Heath was holding her, and they were both laughing.

'Do you know what I think?' he said as she gasped for breath. Without waiting for her answer, he turned the shower off and, yanking her close, he kissed her—and this time there was no brushing, or teasing, or delay. They were hungry for each other and Heath kissed her in a way she had never been kissed before—in a way no one would ever kiss her again. He made her feel powerful and sexy and safe and more at risk than she had ever been in her life.

Life was a risk.

Love was a risk.

Was she going to spend all her life dreaming?

When Heath pulled back she waited. She was expecting the worst—planning for it—trying to work out how she could stalk out of his house with her head held high in soaking wet clothes. 'Not against the wall,' he murmured, his face creasing in a smile as he stared down at her.

'Been there—done that?' Bronte's brows rose.

She laughed softly against his face as Heath swung her into his arms, and then protested, 'We can't,' when Heath carried her straight out of the bathroom and into his bedroom.

'I can do what I like in my own house.'

'We'll make the bed wet.'

'You can count on it,' Heath promised as he stripped off his clothes.

'No,' he said when she started to do the same, 'that's my job.'

He undressed her slowly, kissing her naked flesh as he removed each garment with the utmost care. It was like the first time for her, Bronte thought as Heath stared down.

Bronte's naked body was a revelation to him—everything in miniature. It was the most beautiful thing he had ever seen—a work of art. She brought out the best in him. She made him draw on tenderness he hadn't known he possessed. He had always expressed physical emotions in a very different way. He embraced her gently, wanting nothing more than to protect her, and to forget all the reasons why he shouldn't be making love to her.

This was a moment out of time for both of them, a moment to give and receive pleasure, though she was so small against him—he couldn't believe what had happened in the kitchen at Hebers Ghyll. That had been a mindless frenzy, the result of years of pent-up need for both of them, but this was different...better. He could take his time and draw it out for both of them. And however fierce she was—and Bronte could be fierce—he would only use a fraction of his strength in response—and even the thought of that self-imposed curb aroused him.

'You're holding back,' she accused him, emerald fire blazing out of rapidly darkening eyes, 'and I want all your attention—'

'And you shall have it,' he promised, moving down the bed.

'I'm not complaining,' she hurried to assure him when he eased her legs over his shoulders. 'I'll never complain again.'

And as she groaned with pleasure he parted her lips and gave her his undivided attention for a considerable amount of time.

Her world exploded in a starburst of crystalline sensation, like firework night with constant repeats, Bronte thought as she heard herself exclaiming with guttural appreciation again and again. When she came to enough to take account of her surroundings and what she was doing, it was to find Heath cradling her in his arms. 'Oh...'

'Oh?' His lips tugged up as he dropped a kiss on her mouth. 'More?'

'What do you think?' she said, gasping as his hand found her.

'I think you've been missing this,' Heath said, easing her over the edge again with a few well-judged passes of his forefinger. 'That's it, baby...let yourself go,' he instructed, cupping her buttocks to hold her in place as she bucked and screamed for what seemed like for ever.

For two people who had decided absolutely that this must never happen, they were making a very good fist of it, Bronte thought wryly as Heath moved on top of her. 'You're so much bigger than me.'

'Somewhat,' Heath agreed wryly. 'I like that you sound so thankful.'

'Oh, believe me, I am...'

'Wider,' Heath murmured.

'Is that an instruction?' she challenged, giving Heath one of her looks as he pressed her knees back.

'What do you think?'

'I think I'm going to like this...'

'I think we both are.'

She cried out softly as he eased inside her. Filling her completely, he rested still for a moment, and when he began to move it was slow and deep, and all the while he was holding her in his arms and making love to her, Heath was kissing her, gently and tenderly, and with such a look in his eyes, Bronte wondered if anyone before them had known anything like this. She was so turned on by the extremes of pleasure it was almost inevitable her teeth would sink into him at some point.

'Wildcat,' Heath accused her, tumbling Bronte onto her back. And then they were rolling and tumbling and wrestling, until they managed to play-fight their way off the bed.

Lucky for them, there was a well-placed rug—lucky for Bronte when Heath cushioned her fall. 'This relationship relies far too much on my landing on you,' she said, pretending disapproval as she raised herself up on her forearms to stare down into his face.

'I just move faster than you do.' He grinned up.

'Your reflexes are perfectly tuned,' she agreed with satisfaction. 'I couldn't improve on them if I tried.' And with a contented sigh she nuzzled her face against his shoulder.

He caressed her, stroking her hair, knowing Bronte had a permanent place in his life even if it was impossible to see how those pieces could ever fit together. He would never mislead her. He would never promise Bronte anything he couldn't deliver.

'You feel so good,' she whispered, turning her head to kiss him gently on the chin. 'You're a marshmallow beneath all those beer cans and motorbike parts.'

'Don't break your teeth on this marshmallow,' he warned. 'I'm no Prince Charming, Bronte.'

'More Alaric the Visigoth? I love Visigoths,' she assured him, and then he was kissing her again, and she was kissing him back, and the future with all its complications faded away.

Heath's rough hands on her buttocks were so firm and thrilling, and yet they could turn so gentle when he was caressing her breasts. His fingers knew just how to torment her nipples and his hands were more than persuasive when he used them to cup her face to kiss her. She had never thought to be kissed like this—to be kissed by Heath like this. He made her feel as if anything were possible, as if she could feel this way for ever…

For ever starts tonight, Bronte thought, writhing in

ecstasy on the bed beneath Heath. And when he thrust one powerful thigh between her legs she refused to listen to the cynic inside her who insisted feelings as strong as this couldn't possibly last.

'Are you okay?' Heath murmured when she gasped as if in pain.

'Never better,' she said fiercely, and, staring into his eyes, she wrapped her legs even more tightly around his waist.

'Relax,' Heath soothed, pulling back.

Heath was so gentle with her it stoked her hunger until, refusing to suffer any more delay, she thrust her hips, claiming him, and only then did she see the slow smile on Heath's lips suggesting that was exactly what he had planned for her to do.

This slow, lazy way of making love was incredible. Breathing steadily instead of hectically, she was able to appreciate the sensation of being stretched and filled so completely, fully for the first time. She had always been in such a rush before.

'Are you okay?' Heath murmured when she thrashed her head on the pillow in extremes of pleasure.

'Your fault,' she gasped. 'You're so big.'

'Fault?' Heath queried, his lips curving with amusement. 'I've never heard it called that before.'

'I'm not complaining. I just have to get used to it each time,' she told him, lacing her fingers through his thick dark hair.

'I'm going to slow you down,' Heath told her when the urge became too great and she tried to hurry him.

'No,' she complained, increasing her grip on him, working muscles even she hadn't known she had.

'Yes,' Heath argued, and then he worked his hips— and not just back and forth with a compelling and irresistible rhythm, but from side to side, massaging persuasively until she screamed out her release in his arms.

'Better?' Heath murmured against her mouth.

'The best ever,' she groaned, still pulsing with pleasure and holding him in place.

That grip was all it took to make him hard again. They were good together. They were outstanding. He moved in response to Bronte's fierce instruction— hard—fast—deep. He could do that. With pleasure.

'Do you realise we've rocked the rug from one side of the room to the other?' he asked her some time later. 'I think it's time we took this to the bed.'

'You won't find any argument from me,' Bronte assured him, laughing against his mouth. Scooping her up, he carried her across the room.

'Do you think you'll ever get tired?' she said when he lowered her onto the sheets.

'I'll let you know,' he said. Slipping a pillow beneath her hips, he raised her up into an even more receptive position, and, taking his cue, she gripped the bed rail above her head.

'You're fantastic,' she cried out as another wave of pleasure hit her. Before she had time to recover, he turned her so she was kneeling in front of him with her hips held high. Holding her in place with one hand, he teased her into a frenzy of excitement with the other as he moved inside her to the rhythm he knew she liked best.

They must have fallen asleep with exhaustion, because she woke to find Heath watching her as she slept. 'What?' she whispered.

'You,' he murmured, barely moving his lips as he eased his head on the pillow.

'Me?'

'You…Bronte—'

'Don't say it,' she told him, putting her finger over his lips.

'I have to.'

'No, you don't. I know we live different lives. I know your life is here in London, Heath, and I'm glad I came down. I'll be able to picture you now.' She'd be able to hold it in her heart, Bronte thought. 'This was just one of those crazy episodes,' she said, 'for both of us.'

'And you're okay with that?' Heath said, frowning.

'I'm okay with that. We can still be friends. I mean—we're sophisticated adults, aren't we?'

Heath smiled his slow, sexy smile, but his gaze was somewhere else. 'We're adults,' he agreed.

'Okay,' she said softly, kissing his chest. 'So here's what we're going to do. No—this time, I'm setting the agenda, Heath,' Bronte insisted when Heath started to say something. 'You have to let me do this.' She waited a moment. 'You've got that copy of my contract. So—I'm going to take a shower now, and then I'm going to get dressed, call a cab—and go home.' There, she'd got it out. Her voice sounded a little wobbly, but still determined. Tilting her chin at the old defiant angle, she added, 'Anything else would be unbearable—so, please don't say anything. You're not allowed to speak.'

She slipped out of bed before Heath could argue. Dragging a cover around herself, she headed for the bathroom. It was over, this…little interlude. It was already in the memory box where the dreamweaver would take care of it.

She got the cab to drop her at the office first so she could pick up her things. She cried all the way. The cabby passed back a box of tissues without a word. No doubt he had seen this sort of thing before. She couldn't cry when she got back to Hebers Ghyll with the good news and spoil it for everyone. She couldn't cry at Heath's office in front of Quentin, who'd been so kind to her. And she definitely couldn't cry in front of Heath. 'Thank you,' she said, handing over a large tip when she got out of the cab.

'Look at it this way, love,' the cabbie advised. 'It can only get better from here.'

'Yeah—sure you're right,' she agreed, rustling up a smile. Thanking the cabbie and saying goodbye, she tipped her chin and put on her ready-to-see-Quentin face.

Quentin was subdued. Had Heath spoken to him already—asked him to have everything ready for her?

'Things didn't exactly go to plan, did they?' Quentin remarked.

'They went exactly to plan,' Bronte argued. 'I just left too much stuff out of the plan.'

'The devil's in the detail,' Quentin agreed.

'He certainly is. But, Quentin, the good news is, I got the job—thanks to you,' Bronte added, giving a surprised Quentin a hug. 'So I have to get back—there's a job waiting for me and people I want to share the good news with that Heath is keeping the estate.'

'Great,' Quentin drawled without much enthusiasm. 'Say hello to the country for me.'

'Why don't you come and say hello to it yourself?' Bronte suggested from the door.

Quentin grimaced. 'Like Heath, the thought of all that fresh air and organic food makes me wince.'

'I'm sure I could persuade you to change your mind.'

She refused to think about Heath. 'If you do decide to give it a try, you know where to find me.'

'Yes,' Quentin agreed witheringly, 'in a hay barn dressed in dungarees.'

'Not until next September. Until Harvest Home, then—'

'Harvest Home?' she heard Quentin scoff as she shut the door, but she could see him smiling through the glass.

CHAPTER FIFTEEN

CHRISTMAS came and went, and to everyone's disappointment the hall wasn't ready in time for the party. Bronte buried her disappointment in renewed effort. Not seeing Heath since she left him in London hurt most of all, but she remained in regular contact by phone and e-mail—and it was all very businesslike, which left her feeling hollow. Other than that, her efforts to bring the land back from the brink took up all her time, just the way she liked it. With the healthy proceeds from the fresh produce and the happy chickens she was able to take on more people from the village. Somehow she managed to find time to cook too. She considered that a pleasure—a reward for her hard-working team at the end of each back-breaking day. She had even been persuaded by the local authority to take on some disaffected youths on short-term contracts. With the proviso that they came with trained staff, how could she refuse, when each one that passed through the gates reminded her of the first time she'd met Heath?

Easter came and went and there was still no sign of Heath, though they exchanged e-mails and she delivered her report to him as agreed each Friday. But e-mails were cold, impersonal things, and she worried how easily they could be misunderstood. Their video conferences were almost as bad. Heath was always in such a hurry to get away.

'It's a compliment,' Colleen insisted. 'You're doing such a good job Heath doesn't need to interfere.'

Bronte laughed. 'Apart from his phone calls every day, twice a day, do you mean?'

'At least he calls,' Colleen pointed out. 'He must like speaking to you.'

'Heath wants to check up on progress,' Bronte argued as they cleared up after breakfast. 'I just wish—' She stopped herself just in time.

'You miss him,' Colleen supplied.

Bronte shrugged. 'This is Heath's property, not mine. I just think he should show more interest—do more than call.'

'Heath's a busy man, Bronte—and even if he does want to spend more time here, he'll have to plan for it—fit it in—and all that takes time.'

'It's been almost a year.'

'It's been nine months.'

'Okay,' Bronte conceded wryly. 'I could have had a baby in that time.'

'No way am I getting into that,' Colleen told her with a wave of her hand, heading out.

As summer ripened into its full splendour Bronte joined the workers in the fields. She came back most days exhausted, but content. Heath's team had worked wonders on the old buildings, and had even started work on the castle, while Bronte's team, which had expanded to include the local authority boys as well as some school leavers, had worked wonders with the harvest.

This was what Uncle Harry must have had in mind, Bronte reflected as she watched the last of the hay bales being dumped off the back of the harvester. The sky was a clear scrubbed blue with only a wisp of cloud, and the scent of fertile earth was unbelievably intoxicating. It was as if the summer sun had warmed the earth for just this moment, producing a scent Bronte only wished she could bottle and share.

She planned to give everyone a day off so they could sleep in tomorrow. Harvesting could be a tricky business if the weather was unpredictable, but it had been dry for days and promised to remain so—even so they'd worked like stink in case the weather changed. Their reward was plain to see. It wouldn't be every year that they would be able to contemplate a full hay barn as well as having spare stock to sell.

She looked like a regular land girl, Bronte mused as she strode back happily towards her cottage. Gone were the purple leggings and flimsy top, and in their place were the dungarees Quentin had mocked.

Quentin…Bronte smiled as she remembered Heath's PA, and then her thoughts turned inevitably to Heath. Why didn't he come? Why didn't the ache for him lessen? Some days she doubted it ever would. Instead of thinking about herself, she should be thinking about rewarding everyone for their hard work, Bronte reflected as she stood by the stile, dragging on the warm air and staring over the golden carpet of cut wheat. Heath wasn't here to do it, so she would do something special. They might have missed the Christmas party, but there was no reason why they couldn't have a party now. Why not have that Harvest Home she had teased Quentin about— invite everyone from the village? Invite Quentin—

And Heath?

And Heath.

She told her inner voice to be quiet now. That was

quite enough nonsense for one day and there was some important planning to be done.

Heath couldn't come. Why wasn't she surprised? But he'd send a representative, he promised Bronte during their regular Friday hook-up.

'Hi, doll—' Quentin appeared briefly at Heath's shoulder before hurrying away.

'Hi, Quentin.'

'Make it a good party,' Heath insisted, 'and don't forget to send me the bills.'

'I wi—' Was as far as she got before Heath cut the connection. 'And I'll be sure to attach some photographs to my next mail so you can see how much fun we had without you,' she assured the blank screen with a lump like a brick in her throat.

It was the perfect day for the perfect event. The sun had beaten down all week and the castle, with its newly renovated staterooms, would be open to the public for the first time. They had just managed to get the last bales of hay into the barn before everyone had to dash back home to get ready for the party. As well as dancing and a feast provided by Bronte, there was going to be a cake stall on the lawn leading down to the lake, as well as hoopla, a bran tub, and a bric-a-brac table. Colleen had gone the whole nine yards, dressing up as a fortune teller, complete with huge gold earrings and a headscarf, which she'd plucked from her normal accessory box, she told Bronte. And Bronte, feeling sick of the sight of the cakes she had been baking non-stop, had put herself in charge of the water-bomb stocks where the local head teacher had gamely offered to be pelted to raise money for charity. The bunting was flying, the band was tuning up, and the first of the guests were due to arrive within the hour. Bronte did her final check, wondering if she dared relax. Surely, nothing could go wrong now. Everything was ready for the party of the year, so now all she had to do was change her clothes.

He saw the red glow in the sky when they were still miles away.

'What's that?' Quentin said, peering out of the window. 'I thought you didn't get light pollution in the country?'

'You don't,' Heath said, stamping down on the gas.

The party was cancelled. Of course it was cancelled. Bronte was too busy forming everyone up in a line so they could pass buckets of water from the lake to the source of the fire to even remember she had once planned a party. If she'd had time to think about it she would have said she was numb, but right now she was all logic and fierce determination to save what she could.

The line of people stretched from the lake to the barn. She'd made the call to the local fire department and, with a heavy heart, to the police, and now all she could do was tag onto the line and help to pass the buckets until the fire service arrived.

The Lamborghini skidded to a halt. Throwing the door open, he ran. Wherever Bronte was, he was sure she'd be in the thick of it. Why the hell had he stayed away so long?

Because he never took holidays—because everything took time to arrange—

To hell with that—he should have been here sooner.

The smoke choked him as he grew closer to the fire.

His eyes stung, and fear clung to him with the same tenacity as the claggy filth of oily soot. He only realised now how fierce the fire was, and what a hold it had taken on the barn. Nothing could be saved, though a squadron of firefighters had high-powered hoses trained on it. He could feel Bronte's despair above the heat of burning hay and stink of choking smoke. He blamed himself for not following his instincts. Life, business, money, success, what did any of it mean without Bronte? The instant he'd been told what she'd done—starting slowly with some of the local, out-of-work youths, and then growing in confidence, until she was persuaded by the local authority to take on boys like him—boys like he'd been. If anyone knew what a mistake that was for a girl on her own, he did. The moment he'd heard where this new intake was coming from he'd dropped everything—but not soon enough. He knew what they were capable of, but Bronte steadfastly refused to see the harm in anyone. Glass half full, that was Bronte. But optimism and determination couldn't save her from this. He'd thought that by making a clean break it would give her space to fly, but she wouldn't fly far with her wings burned off.

He shielded his face against the heat. An officer told him to move back. He explained he was the owner of the estate and asked if anyone knew where his estate manager was. Bronte had called them, he was told, but no one had seen her since.

His darting gaze swept the crowd. Where was she? Then Colleen found him and told him about Bronte arranging the line of buckets while they waited for the engines to arrive. 'Have you seen her?' he demanded.

Colleen shook her head. 'Not since then.'

Colleen looked defeated. 'Go back to the kitchen,'

he ordered. 'Make tea—lots of it—strong and sweet. Everyone will need some.'

'I'll do that,' she said, looking grateful that he'd found her a task.

Bronte would get her water for the buckets from the lake, he reasoned, and the lake was at the back of the barn.

'You can't go there,' someone shouted at him.

He was conveniently deaf.

The best he expected to find was Bronte broken and sobbing on the ground. The worst he refused to think about.

As ever, she surprised him. He found her in the stable yard with her back braced against a stable door while the occupants she'd trapped inside were trying their best to kick it down. His relief at finding her unharmed was indescribable. His feelings at seeing her again were off the scale. 'What the hell are you doing?' Lifting her out of the way, he took her place. At the sound of his raised voice the kicking stopped abruptly.

'I saw them set fire to the barn,' she said, wiping a smoke-begrimed hand across her face. 'If I moved from here I thought there was a chance they could get out and get away—'

'They?'

'Two of them,' she explained.

'You imprisoned two grown men?' he exclaimed.

'They're just boys,' she said, flashing him a glance.

He swore viciously. 'This is my fault—I put this idea in your head. You should have waited for me to initiate a scheme like this.'

'What?' she fired back. 'Like wait for ever?'

He slammed his head back against the door in frustration. The sound echoed in the courtyard above the

shouted instructions of the firefighters and the police.
She was right. He should have been here sooner. This
was his responsibility, not Bronte's. 'I'll call the police,'
he said, bringing out his phone.

'Everything happened faster than the boys expected,'
Bronte explained as he cut the line. 'The barn went up
like a rocket, and there was no time for them to get away
before the police arrived, and so they hid in here. I just
dropped the latch.'

'You shouldn't have chased them.'

'What did you expect me to do? Stand around sulking
because the party was cancelled?'

She was furious and he deserved it. Emotion welled
inside him. 'I only care that you're safe,' he shouted, his
voice hoarse with smoke and emotion.

They were silent for a moment, and then she said
quietly, 'Hello, Heath.'

He shook his head, then held her gaze. 'Hello,
Bronte...'

All the things he should have said to her long before
now. All the things he should have done for her. His
head was pressed against the door and as he turned to
stare down at her he wondered what kind of fool he'd
been. The door she'd been defending was one of the
few yet to be replaced and the rotten wood was already
splintering under the barrage of blows it had received.
They could have killed her. 'Would you like to go and
get changed for the party now? I'll deal with this.'

'The party's cancelled,' she said steadily, 'and I'm
not leaving you.'

'I was hoping you'd say that.' He glanced at the petrol
can lying discarded in the centre of the yard, and the box
of matches Bronte had tightly clutched in her hand.

'It's all gone,' she whispered.

'Don't,' he said firmly. 'This isn't over yet. We'll build a new barn—we can buy in more hay—'

'But we didn't need to buy hay before this happened.'

'And now we do,' he told her calmly. 'All businesses have setbacks, Bronte. It's how you get over them that matters.' There were oily smudges on her face. Her eyes were red and wounded from the smoke, and from crying, he suspected—not that Bronte would show that sort of weakness in a crisis situation. 'You're quite a girl,' he murmured.

'And you're still an absentee landlord.' She scowled, rallying.

'Something I'll have to change.'

She didn't believe him. Why should she? Now wasn't the time, but it might be the only chance he got. 'I have a mature business, and when I realised what I was missing out on I think I finally learned to delegate. I've appointed a CEO, an operating officer, a financial controller, and a sales and marketing guy.'

'To do your one job,' she said. She didn't dare to hope that this might mean progress. 'No wonder you're such a pain in the ass, Heath.'

'They should be able to handle it,' he said wryly.

'While you take broader control of your business portfolio, which now includes a country estate?'

'I'm only sorry it's taken so long,' he said, 'but it takes time to find the right person.'

'And less than an hour to undo a full year's work,' Bronte remarked as she glanced over her shoulder to where the flames were still hungrily licking up the remains of the barn.

'We'll get over it,' Heath promised.

'We?'

'You and me. We'll get over this. I promise—'

'Together?'

He placed another call to the police. 'Go and hurry them along, will you, while I bring these lads out?'

'Don't take any unnecessary risks, Heath.'

'Thanks for the advice.' He flashed a rueful grin. 'I think I'll be okay. And if I'm not, I'll call for you.'

A faint smile touched Bronte's red-rimmed eyes. 'I'll be right back,' she said, starting to run.

He wanted a chance to speak to the boys without anyone being present. He wanted to see them punished and for them to make reparation for what they'd done, but he wanted them to know there was another way—if they chose to take it. He wanted them to spread the word when they went inside that there was someone who understood the poison that drove them and who had the antidote to it, and that this same individual would be running the boot camp at Hebers Ghyll.

CHAPTER SIXTEEN

HEATH worked like a Trojan alongside the officers to clear the debris and make everywhere safe, while the people who could stayed on to help. Bronte was touched to find Quentin in the kitchen making tea and sandwiches for everyone, and didn't even mind that he had taken command of her beloved Aga.

'I've never had such a huge piece of kit to play with before. Or so many interesting new friends in uniform.'

'Quentin,' Bronte scolded, knowing that if anyone could bring a smile to people's faces when they most needed it, it was this man.

'What's wrong?' Heath said, drawing Bronte aside discreetly. 'You've been so brave up to now. Don't crumple on me, Bronte.'

'I'm not crumpling,' she said, pushing him away. 'I'm just watching you and Quentin, and all the people milling round the kitchen, and wishing it could stay like this for ever. I know,' she said through gritted teeth before Heath had chance to speak. 'I know I'm dreaming again.'

He was too tired to argue. Everyone was tired and battle scarred, but he had to admit Quentin had come up trumps, making people laugh as he doled out mugs of tea and coffee, and the biggest, thickest sandwiches, which everyone professed to love. But it was to Bronte that most of the praise was due, Heath reflected as he watched her moving between people, offering her own brand of encouragement. She had worked tirelessly inside and outside the house, clearing up the mess, and offering words of reassurance, creating such a feeling of warmth and camaraderie that everyone wanted to stay on late to help out.

'You should try one of Quentin's sandwiches,' she said, distracting him by plonking a huge platter in front of his nose. 'They're really great.'

'And he's used to having them made for him,' Heath said, selecting one. 'Quentin's partner is a dab hand in the kitchen—with a penchant for gourmet food.'

'Lucky Quentin.'

'Lucky me,' he said.

They were too busy to speak after that. Bronte didn't go home with the rest of the crowd, but stayed on to help Quentin and Heath clean up the kitchen. It was like the day after a party when everything was set to rights… except there'd been no party. And now there was no barn, she thought wistfully, staring out of the window at the heap of jagged timbers and blackened ash.

'Don't go home tonight,' Heath murmured, coming up behind her.

She turned in his arms. I can't go through this again, she thought. The others had left the kitchen and all any of them were seeking tonight was comfort, but where would comfort lead with Heath? She wondered what to say to him, how to phrase what she had to say to him—to a man who had led so much of the salvage work today. I'm not in the mood, sounded ugly. I don't want to spend the night with you, would be a lie.

'I'm not going to let you go home to an empty cottage,' Heath said. 'I want you to stay here with me, Bronte.'

'I don't think that's a very good idea.'

Heath's smoke-blackened face creased in his trademark grin. 'I'll run you a bath—'

'Heath, I—'

'And I'll call you when it's ready.'

She could argue, or she could accept Heath's kindness for once. She could soak in soapy bubbles, which right now seemed an irresistible option.

She listened to Heath bounding up the stairs and marvelled at his energy. After everything they'd been through she couldn't have felt more exhausted. She supposed it was the knowledge that everything everyone had worked so hard to achieve had gone up in flames. What was the point—?

She was so wrong, Bronte thought as she caught sight of Quentin's neatly folded drying cloth hanging on the Aga rail. It was such a little thing amongst the monumental happenings of the night, but it showed Quentin cared. So many people had cared tonight, and if all that goodwill could be harvested there wasn't the slightest possibility that Herbers Ghyll would go to the wall.

Heath didn't call downstairs, he came downstairs to make sure she hadn't changed her mind. 'And I'm going to stand outside the door to make sure you're all right,' he said, 'and I won't take any argument. You just yell if you need me.'

'But you're tired too,' she said, gazing up at Heath's grimy face. 'You must be. You go and clean up—or aren't you planning to wash tonight?'

'It'll keep,' he said. 'When I know you're safely

tucked in bed I'll take a shower and clean this dirt off then.'

'Thank you,' she said softly, meeting Heath's gaze.

'There's no need to thank me,' he told her as he opened the bathroom door. 'And there's no hurry, either. You take your time.'

The hard man had laid out some towels for her, and also one of his robes and a T-shirt, both of which would drown her. She appreciated the gesture more than she could say. He'd even filled the bath with warm, soapy water. She climbed in and sank beneath the surface, wondering if she would ever be clean again.

She washed the filth from her hair and her face, and then took one last quick soak, conscious that Heath must be equally exhausted, however he appeared. Getting out of the bath, she dried herself, and put on the T-shirt and robe, wrapping her hair in a towel.

Heath was waiting as she came out of the bathroom, and, putting his arm around her shoulders, he led her into his bedroom. She was swallowed up in the huge double bed. The pillows were soft and the sheets held the faint scent of sunshine and lavender. He tucked the sheets up to her chin, and kissed her forehead. 'Sleep,' he murmured.

She didn't need any encouragement.

She woke in the night to find Heath lying beside her. *Wearing boxers.* She smiled. He was holding her in his arms. 'You cried out,' he said, stroking her hair back from her face.

'Sorry.'

'Don't be.' Kissing her again, he drew her close until she fell asleep wrapped in his arms.

Heath had gone by the time she woke up, leaving Bronte to wonder if she'd been dreaming. She'd certainly overslept, she realised, glancing groggily at the clock. And she had work to do.

Heaving herself out of bed, still half asleep, she staggered to the bathroom for a wake-up shower. She wasn't worried about where Heath was. He'd be here at Hebers Ghyll setting things right. There was nothing more certain in her mind.

When she came downstairs the yard was full of builders' vans and it seemed everyone from the village had come to help. And driving towards them was the biggest truck Bronte had ever seen, with huge prefabricated wooden sides and struts fixed onto the back of it with ropes. 'What's happening?' she exclaimed with excitement, bursting through the door.

'Come and see,' Colleen cried, grabbing hold of Bronte's arm and dragging her along.

Heath was standing on the girders putting a heavy beam into place with the boys who hadn't been involved in starting the fire helping him. Apparently oblivious to the cold, he was wearing his old worn ripped jeans and a tight-fitting top that could have been any colour it was so blackened by grime and dust, but he was setting a good example to the boys with his hard hat, work gloves, and steel-capped boots.

Bronte felt so proud as she stared up at him. Everything had come full circle to its rightful place. Everything they had ever talked about flashed through her head—everything they'd ever done together—everything they'd learned about each other. And while that circle had been turning and becoming whole again, she thought about the journey they'd travelled. And the fun they'd had—the rows too, not to mention the frantic, fabulous sex…as well as the slow, sensual love-making. Right up to last night when Heath had held her in his arms as she slept, and had just been there for her, watching over her, silent and protective.

As if he felt her staring up at him, Heath looked down. He hadn't shaved this morning. Heath was a man on a mission—a man in his most deliciously unreconstructed state. Their eyes met briefly. It was all Heath had time for before he hefted the beam into place.

'I'm going to go and get breakfast started,' Bronte told Colleen, who was a gem for bringing her clean clothes from the cottage.

'Lunch,' Colleen said with a laugh. 'It's almost noon.'

'Why didn't you wake me?'

'Heath said you should sleep—and everyone agreed. No one worked harder than you last night, Bronte—and no one blames you for sleeping in. No one lost more,' Colleen added when Bronte started to argue.

'Heath lost more. You lost more. I don't think I lost anything,' Bronte murmured as she turned to take one last look at Heath directing his team. 'We'll keep the excess hay,' she told Colleen as they walked back to the kitchen. 'We won't sell it as we'd planned to—instead we'll use it to restock the new barn.'

Heath was right, Bronte thought as she continued explaining her plans. All businesses suffered setbacks, but what had happened here, however dramatic and irreversible it had seemed at the time, was still something they could get round.

She was back, Heath thought, rejoicing as he towelled down roughly after his shower. Bronte was back, and firing on all cylinders. He'd seen it in her eyes when she came to watch the new barn being raised. She had recovered her fighting sprit. He'd felt it then, and he felt it now, that huge surge of something he now accepted was love. He'd fought it, ignored it, scorned it, and trampled it—whenever he'd got half a chance. But now he craved it. He wanted Bronte. He wanted Bronte to love him as he loved her, and he wanted to build a lot more than a barn with her.

The fire had been a terrible disaster, but out of it had come a reckoning of things that were important in life—things that could be rebuilt, regenerated, or reclaimed, and those that could never be. If Bronte had been harmed in any way he would never have forgiven himself. If the worst had happened, which he wouldn't even think about, no amount of determination in the world would bring her back to him. And now they had got to know each other all over again he doubted Bronte's nature could be ruined by anything—even him, because there was steel beneath that quirky daintiness, and fire beneath those caring, dreamy eyes.

He had even shaved. Leaning on the sink, he stared at himself in the mirror, wondering if this new fierce passion would be as easy to turn into victory as expressing powerful feelings with his fists had been. He thought not. Bronte was tricky. She could never be called predictable. But he was ready for her. Straightening up, he reached for a towel and patted his temporarily smooth cheeks. His thick hair refused to dry however much he towelled it. He slicked it back roughly with his hands. Time was a-wasting. He fastened his shirt as he headed downstairs, though, unusually, he paused to take a deep breath outside the kitchen door.

Blind to anything else in the room he only saw Bronte standing in front of the Aga. Apron tied round her waist and knotted in front, she was dressed in purple leggings and a flimsy top. The flip-flops and toe rings had been reinstated and her hair was hanging in crazy tangles to her waist. She had never looked lovelier—though that might have had something to do with the huge tray of delicious-looking food she was holding in hands—tiny hands—currently concealed beneath huge black oven mitts.

'I love you,' he announced, walking straight up to her.

Taking the gloves and the tray in one slick move, he put them aside. And then, because he was so tall and she was so tiny, he knelt at her feet holding both her tiny hands in his. 'I love you more than anything in the world.'

He only realised when he heard the raucous applause that they weren't alone, but nothing was going to distract him from his purpose. He waited for the noise to die down, and then he asked her clearly and steadily, 'Will you marry me, Bronte?' She hadn't said a word up to now, and he was in no way confident of the outcome.

Then she knelt too. Or maybe her legs gave way with shock.

'That wasn't supposed to happen,' he said, looking down. 'I'm supposed to be the supplicant here.'

'Better we face each other for this,' she said. 'I love you too,' she said simply. 'I've always loved you, Heath, and I always will.'

'But you haven't answered my question,' he pointed out.

'Patience,' she told him. 'I'm just getting to that.' Breathless silence surrounded them, which was released in a shiver of sighs when she added, 'Heath, that was the most romantic proposal any girl could receive.'

'And?' he demanded impatiently.

'Of course I'll marry you,' Bronte whispered as the kitchen exploded in a frenzy of cheers.

He wanted to give Bronte something very special to show how much he loved her—but what to give the girl who had everything? Bronte had nothing in a material sense, but she didn't want anything. Nothing he could buy her with money would mean a thing—she'd rather have a good load of quality manure to spread on her precious vegetable garden. He'd had to think laterally and go that extra mile...

And so he did. Swinging out of the Jeep just before Christmas, he dragged Bronte into his arms. They were getting married at the end of the week, so his timing had never been more important.

'Okay, Mr Mysterious,' she said, trying to peer inside the cab. 'What are you hiding in there?'

'Not what. Who...'

There was a pause, and then she said, 'Mum? Dad?'

He left them to it. He had been introduced to emotions, but they still weren't his best friend.

Bronte had her own way of thanking him. He was okay with that. Sunshine was streaming through the curtains by the time they could talk coherently. 'You're an excellent student,' he murmured as she dozed in his arms, 'if a little hasty sometimes.'

'Practice makes perfect—and seeing as I've got a lot more practice ahead of me...'

'Presents first,' he said, reminding her of their arrangement. 'You said you have something for me—and I've certainly got something for you.'

'You certainly have,' she said, punching him playfully.

She thought back to the youth Heath had been and the

man he had become, and just hoped she'd got it right. 'I hope you like it,' she said.

'I'm sure I will. Whatever you've chosen will be perfect—it had better be,' he teased her as she leaned out of bed to retrieve the tiny package she'd hidden away from him. 'Did you use a whole roll of sticky tape on this?' he said as he picked it open.

Freed from its wrappings, the small wooden chess piece lay in his palm. He stared at it for a long time.

'I do have the rest of them,' Bronte reassured him, 'and I found the board in the attic, as well as the table you used to play chess on with Uncle Harry. I had them renovated—they're downstairs. I would have given them to you—'

Heath stopped her with a kiss, and from his expression when he pulled away Bronte knew she'd got it very right indeed.

'That's the most thoughtful gift anyone's ever given me,' he admitted. 'And now I've got something for you…'

'What's this?' Bronte said, frowning when Heath handed over a large manila envelope. 'Is it another contract? A permanent one?'

'Why don't you open it and find out?' Heath suggested.

Tearing the envelope open, she started to read, and as she did her expression was slowly changing from interest into shock. 'Heath, you can't do this.'

'Why can't I?' Heath said. 'Hebers Ghyll is mine to do with as I like—so why can't I give half to you?'

'Be serious, Heath,' Bronte exclaimed, laughing as she shook her head, 'You can't just hand over half of an estate like Hebers Ghyll.'

'I expect you to take half the responsibility for it.'

'Of course, and I'd love to do that, but—'

'No buts,' he said. 'It's done.'

'Are you sure?' Bronte murmured, still not able to believe what Heath was giving her.

'Never more so,' he assured her. 'Oh—and there's something else. I've been carrying this around all evening.'

What a great sight, Bronte thought as Heath leaned out of bed to rumble in the pocket of his jeans. 'Just stay there,' she said. 'That's a good enough gift for me right there.'

'What?' Heath said as he swung back to join her. Narrowing his eyes, he gave Bronte a stern look. 'Were you staring at my butt?'

'As if I would.'

'I might have to punish you,' he warned.

'Please.'

'Okay, your punishment is to wear this on every occasion—even in the stables when you're mucking out.'

'What is it?'

'Guess,' Heath said dryly, handing over the small red velvet box.

It was one of those 'don't dare to hope moments', but she did dare. She had always dared, or she wouldn't be here, Bronte thought as Heath raised a brow.

'Maybe I'd better put some clothes on before you open it,' he said. 'I feel a little underdressed.'

'You'll do just as you are,' Bronte insisted. Opening the box, she gasped. 'I've changed my mind.'

'You have?'

'You're definitely underdressed. You should be wearing running gear—no way am I giving this back.' Removing a ruby the size of a plum surrounded with fabulous brilliant cut diamonds, she allowed Heath to place it on her wedding finger.

'Do you like it?' His eyes were dancing with laughter. 'I realise it's a little bold for someone who lifts hay bales for a living.'

'I'll get round it,' Bronte promised dryly. 'But, seriously, Heath, you didn't need to buy me anything—a piece of cord would do the job just as well.'

'Would you settle for a tent instead of Hebers Ghyll?'

Bronte laughed as Heath drew her into his arms. 'Don't you love it when a plan comes together?'

EPILOGUE

THE wedding was held in the newly renovated Great Hall at Hebers Ghyll a couple of days before Christmas. There was snow on the ground and a great spruce tree stood sentry outside the doors. Decorated with lights and stars and shimmering ribbons, it gave just a hint of the glorious scene inside. The log fire was blazing, and the hall was filled with workmates and friends, Bronte's family and just about everyone from the village. They turned expectantly as she reached the door, but all Bronte could see was Heath, looking like some latter-day Mr Darcy—though much better looking, she thought as the breath caught in her throat. There was a touch of Heathcliff about him too—all that darkly glittering glamour. Heath's hair was just as thick and black and as unruly as ever, though she knew he would have tried to tame it, just as he would have tried to shave so his face remained smooth for longer than five minutes. Both attempts had failed, she was pleased to see, though his tail suit was magnificent and skimmed his powerful frame with loving attention to detail. He must have gone to Quentin's tailor, she guessed as Heath's groomsmen took their place at Heath's side. Not even Quentin had dared to argue when Heath had named Quentin his best man.

The vast, welcoming space was decorated with Christmas flowers—spray roses, aptly named warm heart, crimson hypericum and frosted twigs, vivid gerberas and frowzy amaranthus, and the room was lit by candlelight, which gave the burnished wood panelling an umber glow. The scent of pine and wood smoke in the great stone hearth was such a wonderfully evocative smell, and as Bronte walked in on her father's arm and saw everyone who had helped to make this possible wishing them well she felt she were being carried along on a wave of goodwill.

She had found her dream wedding dress in the city—a simple fall of cream chiffon that floated as she walked, it was cut straight across her breasts and the delicate fabric was swathed and draped over a boned bodice. The gauzy skirt was drawn up on one side over a matt silk Dupion underskirt and had been formed into a delicate camellia on the hip.

Quentin, who had appointed himself wedding-advisor-in-chief, had all but swooned when Bronte had come out of the dressing room wearing this one. 'Perfect,' he'd said. 'We need look no further.' And then he had gusted with relief, because it had taken a solid week of looking for something that wouldn't be too grand, as Bronte put it, but wouldn't look as if she could cut it down to wear with flip-flops and toe rings either.

She had finally, after much argument, given way to Quentin over the veil. She hadn't wanted to wear one, but Quentin had insisted, and so she was wearing a floating three-tiered confection composed of creamy cobwebby net, dusted with the tiniest sparkling diamanté that fell into a long, floating train behind her. Even Bronte had been amazed at how feminine it made her look.

'Tiaras and tattoos?' she had said, laughing when Quentin had agreed she could wear one toe ring.

'Heath wouldn't want you completely changed,' Quentin observed, adding a discreet band of crystals to Bronte's hair while he distracted her.

'Quentin, you're wicked,' she had exclaimed.

'I had the best teacher,' Quentin had informed her and they both knew who he meant.

So now she was walking down the aisle towards the man she loved, dressed by royal appointment—as Quentin insisted she must think of it—in the stratospherically high heels Quentin had chosen for her. 'Heath is so much taller than you,' he had pointed out. 'And I refuse to listen if you start to argue with me.'

The one thing Bronte couldn't argue about was Heath's size. Heath was built on a heroic scale in every department, she thought happily, keeping those thoughts under wraps as she did her best to glide gracefully in front of her bridesmaids, Maisie and Colleen, both of whom were dressed in powder-pink Grecian-style gowns. She was trembling all over by the time she turned to pass her wedding bouquet to Colleen. Lush cream orchids with an intimate flash of purple at their core, the bouquet had been created to Heath's design, and when her father put her hand in Heath's Bronte was sure everyone must have heard her swift intake of breath. At this range he was even more devastating with his stubble-shaded face, and dark, slumberous eyes. The sweeping ebony brows and thick black hair curling rebelliously over the collar of his winged shirt gave him the appearance of some ruthless buccaneer who had sailed into this quiet harbour and taken it by storm—which was pretty much what had happened, Bronte reflected.

'Okay?' Heath whispered, heat and concern mingling in his eyes as he looked at her.

'I am now,' Bronte confirmed, meeting that fiery gaze. Now, if she could just concentrate on the ceremony and put the pleasures of their wedding night out of her mind, she might stand a chance of remembering what she was supposed to say and do.

And then Heath's lips brushed her ear. 'Good,' he murmured, 'because I've got plans for you…'

* * * * *

CLASSIC

Quintessential, modern love stories
that are romance at its finest.

You can find more information on upcoming Harlequin® titles,
free excerpts and more at www.HarlequinInsideRomance.com.

HPECNM0112

REQUEST YOUR
FREE BOOKS!

2 FREE NOVELS PLUS
2 FREE GIFTS!

YES! Please send me 2 FREE Harlequin Presents® novels and my 2 FREE gifts (gifts are worth about $10). After receiving them, if I don't wish to receive any more books, I can return the shipping statement marked "cancel." If I don't cancel, I will receive 6 brand-new novels every month and be billed just $4.30 per book in the U.S. or $4.99 per book in Canada. That's a saving of at least 14% off the cover price! It's quite a bargain! Shipping and handling is just 50¢ per book in the U.S. and 75¢ per book in Canada.* I understand that accepting the 2 free books and gifts places me under no obligation to buy anything. I can always return a shipment and cancel at any time. Even if I never buy another book, the two free books and gifts are mine to keep forever.

106/306 HDN FERQ

Name   (PLEASE PRINT)

Address   Apt. #

City   State/Prov.   Zip/Postal Code

Signature (if under 18, a parent or guardian must sign)

Mail to the **Reader Service:**
IN U.S.A.: P.O. Box 1867, Buffalo, NY 14240-1867
IN CANADA: P.O. Box 609, Fort Erie, Ontario L2A 5X3

Not valid for current subscribers to Harlequin Presents books.

**Are you a current subscriber to Harlequin Presents books
and want to receive the larger-print edition?
Call 1-800-873-8635 or visit www.ReaderService.com.**

* Terms and prices subject to change without notice. Prices do not include applicable taxes. Sales tax applicable in N.Y. Canadian residents will be charged applicable taxes. Offer not valid in Quebec. This offer is limited to one order per household. All orders subject to credit approval. Credit or debit balances in a customer's account(s) may be offset by any other outstanding balance owed by or to the customer. Please allow 4 to 6 weeks for delivery. Offer available while quantities last.

Your Privacy—The Reader Service is committed to protecting your privacy. Our Privacy Policy is available online at www.ReaderService.com or upon request from the Reader Service.

We make a portion of our mailing list available to reputable third parties that offer products we believe may interest you. If you prefer that we not exchange your name with third parties, or if you wish to clarify or modify your communication preferences, please visit us at www.ReaderService.com/consumerschoice or write to us at Reader Service Preference Service, P.O. Box 9062, Buffalo, NY 14269. Include your complete name and address.

USA TODAY bestselling author

Sarah Morgan

brings readers another enchanting story

ONCE A FERRARA WIFE...

When Laurel Ferrara is summoned back to Sicily
by her estranged husband, billionaire
Cristiano Ferrara, Laurel knows things are about
to heat up. And Cristiano's power is a potent
reminder of his Sicilian dynasty's unbreakable rule:
once a Ferrara wife, always a Ferrara wife....

Sparks fly this February

*Louisa Morgan loves being around children.
So when she has the opportunity to tutor bedridden Ellie,
she's determined to bring joy back into the motherless
girl's world. Can she also help Ellie's father open his
heart again? Read on for a sneak peek of*

THE COWBOY FATHER

*by Linda Ford,
available February 2012 from Love Inspired Historical.*

Why had Louisa thought she could do this job? A bubble of self-pity whispered she was totally useless, but Louisa ignored it. She wasn't useless. She could help Ellie if the child allowed it.

Emmet walked her out, waiting until they were out of earshot to speak. "I sense you and Ellie are not getting along."

"Ellie has lost her freedom. On top of that, everything is new. Familiar things are gone. Her only defense is to exert what little independence she has left. I believe she will soon tire of it and find there are more enjoyable ways to pass the time."

He looked doubtful. Louisa feared he would tell her not to return. But after several seconds' consideration, he sighed heavily. "You're right about one thing. She's lost everything. She can hardly be blamed for feeling out of sorts."

"She hasn't lost everything, though." Her words were quiet, coming from a place full of certainty that Emmet was more than enough for this child. "She has you."

"She'll always have me. As long as I live." He clenched his fists. "And I fully intend to raise her in such a way that even if something happened to me, she would never feel like I was gone. I'd be in her thoughts and in her actions every day."

Peace filled Louisa. "Exactly what my father did."

Their gazes connected, forged a single thought about fathers and daughters…how each needed the other. How sweet the relationship was.

Louisa tipped her head away first. "I'll see you tomorrow."

Emmet nodded. "Until tomorrow then."

She climbed behind the wheel of their automobile and turned toward home. She admired Emmet's devotion to his child. It reminded her of the love her own father had lavished on Louisa and her sisters. Louisa smiled as fond memories of her father filled her thoughts. Ellie was a fortunate child to know such love.

Louisa understands what both father and daughter are going through. Will her compassion help them heal—and form a new family? Find out in
THE COWBOY FATHER
by Linda Ford, available February 14, 2012.

Love Inspired Books celebrates 15 years of inspirational romance in 2012! February puts the spotlight on Love Inspired Historical, with each book celebrating family and the special place it has in our hearts. Be sure to pick up all four Love Inspired Historical stories, available February 14, wherever books are sold.

Discover a touching new trilogy from
USA TODAY bestselling author

Janice Kay Johnson

Between Love and Duty

As the eldest brother of three, Duncan MacLachlan
is used to being in control and maintaining an
emotional distance; as a police captain it's his job.
But when he meets Jane Brooks, Duncan soon finds
his control slipping away. Together, they fight for a
young boy's future, and soon Duncan finds himself
hoping to build a future with Jane.

Available February 2012

From Father to Son
(March 2012)

The Call of Bravery
(April 2012)